31 Days of

October

A Haunting Collection Of Hallowe'en Tales

Edited by Glenda Reynolds, Shae Hamrick, and Stephanie Baskerville

Featuring:

Terry Turner

Glenda Reynolds

Andy McKell

C. Baely

Cora Bhatia

db Martin

Elaine Faber

David Russell

Gene Hilgreen

J. Rene Young

Joe Stanley

Lena M. Pate

Lisa M. Collins

Lynette White

Mary Ross

Mirta Oliva

Rebecca Lacy

Elizabeth Ann Boyles

Shae Hamrick

Linda L. Taylor

Sojourner McConnell

Stephanie Baskerville

Christene Britton-Jones

Eric,
Congratulations!
I hope you have
a spooktacular time
Reading the stories.

Sojourner McConnell

~ ~ ~

Book Copyright © 2016 Shae Hamrick
Cover by Glenda Reynolds

ISBN-13: 978-1539087694
ISBN-10: 1539087697

For more information, contact SHamrick Books at
s.hamrick.books@sbglobal.net
Or the Writer's 750 at Goodreads.com

Extended Copyrights Listing

Table of Contents

A note from the Editors and Authors:

Hallowe'en, a mostly North American holiday, is celebrated in the United States of America with costumes, treats, and make believe. It was not always so. There were times in the past that it was the time of the harvest and preparation for winter. Later, the idea of tricks, mischief, magic, and viciousness entered into the night's observance.

In time, after the World Wars, the holiday of Hallowe'en returned as no longer a game of mischief or night of magic, but rather a kids' night of parties and treats traded for avoiding tricks. The mischief was frowned upon and became more of friendly or harmless tricks played on each other. Hallowe'en has become a day to scare one another, dress up as our favorite hero, villain, or some crazy idea such as a credit card machine, and party with other children or adults while enjoying massive quantities of sugary treats and drinks or visiting scary places to get the thrill without the danger.

Along these ends, we would like to provide some stories for your perusal that entertain, raise some hairs on your head, or just plain keep you up at night, looking under the bed.

The stories at the beginning of the book are Hallowe'en themed stories and range from mild to a bit stronger. The stories in the second section are more of the suspenseful and ghostly nature with a touch of humor here and there. And the stories at the end are designed to make you stay up at night thinking about them and wondering if you should turn the lights on … or not.

Thank you for buying this collection and Happy Hallowe'en Everyone.

Hallowe'en Short Stories

A Collection of Tales Fit for Man and Beast.

Icky, Acky Hallowe'en
By Linda L Taylor

Mervin "Icky" Morgan stood at the edge of the sidewalk, his toes almost touching the invisible line which separated the safe and secure part of his way home with the part that went past the cemetery. He sighed. Usually, he could walk this part without flinching. However, tonight of all nights…

He had taken the job at the small grocery store only after reaching an understanding with the owner, Mr. Jamison. Under no circumstances would he work late. He blamed the condition on his mother, who was well known for her frantic concerns over her only child. But the real reason was…he couldn't stand to walk past the cemetery in the dark.

Unfortunately for Icky, circumstances conspired against him this night. Mr. Jamison's daughter had been in a bicycle accident. She didn't seem to be hurt, but the EMTs had taken her to the hospital to be checked over. Mr. Jamison was waiting to take her home.

Then Mark, Icky's relief, had gotten a flat tire on the way to work. When he went to change it, he had found the spare flat as well. He had to wait for a tow. Icky's dad was out of town and his mother had night blindness and wasn't able to drive in the dark. The result? Icky found himself walking home. Alone. In the dark. And worst of all…on Hallowe'en night.

Hallowe'en. All Hallow's Eve. All Saint's Day, when evil spirits and souls of the dead roam the earth. Vampires and zombies and monsters. Icky didn't believe all that stuff. He didn't. Really. And yet…

He eyed the long, long stretch of cement that curved past the graveyard. Normally, he could make it past in just a couple of minutes. But tonight…

Mark's parting words hadn't helped.

"Hey, Ichabod! Be careful walking past that cemetery tonight! Never know when the old Headless Horseman may show up!"

He had laughed right along with everybody else in the store, but that was ten minutes and four blocks ago. Somehow, his steps kept slowing down.

He remembered the first time he had seen that stupid Disney movie, *The Legend of Sleepy Hollow*. He had been in sixth grade. At five feet eight inches, he had already towered over everyone else in his class.

When Ichabod Crane appeared for the first time, Jimmy Kline, the class joker, had turned to Icky and said, "Hey, Mervin! You look just like that guy. Maybe we should start calling you Ichabod!"

The whole class had broken out in laughter, including his teacher who had tried to hide it behind her hand. And the nickname stuck. After five years, he had stopped trying to get rid of it. In fact, he even thought of himself as Icky. It was certainly no worse than Mervin. If only he had filled out a little and didn't still look like that stupid cartoon character. Every Hallowe'en, the teasing started up again. Living in a town called Sleepy Meadows didn't help, either.

But now, before him, was the grave yard.

He took a step onto the sidewalk. That wasn't too bad. He looked at the five trees at the edge of the cemetery. They seemed to be spaced pretty evenly along the way. Maybe if he could just break the trip up into those five small parts, he could make it.

He decided to count his steps on the first part, so he could figure out how many more he had to take before he would make it the whole way across. Two, three, four, concentrating on his feet, he made it to the first tree. Twenty-five steps. That left only a little more than a hundred or so until he was safe on the other side. He could do that. No problem.

Taking a deep breath for courage, he stepped out from behind the safety of that tree. Another step and he laughed. This was gonna be a snap. When he lifted his foot for the next step, he heard a rustling noise. From his right. From the row of graves stones. He didn't want to look over and see what it was. But his eyes rotated that way and dragged the rest of his head unwillingly along.

The leaves on the graves had begun to stir in the light autumn breeze. They whirled and twirled and danced along. Just when he began to relax a little, he noticed a line of twirling leaves heading right for him. He let out a small squeak and half-jumped, half-ran to the safety of the next tree.

Clinging to the other side, he struggled to get his heart to quit trying to jump out of his chest. Finally, his curiosity got the better of him. Had there really been something there? Or had it only been the wind?

Crouching down to make a smaller target, he peered

13

around the edge of the tree, and came face to face with a black, hairy creature. When the mouth yawned open, he saw long, sharp fangs. He never heard the cat's meow as he hightailed it to the next tree. When he looked back, he felt silly for running from a stupid cat, even one as big as that one. However, he had now made it to the third tree. Half way there. Sixty plus more steps.

He took a deep breath and forced one foot to follow the other. Two steps later, a howling suddenly started up. The hair on the back of his neck rose. It sounded like a wolf...or maybe...an evil spirit looking for a victim. When it seemed to be coming closer, he dove for the fourth tree.

Once safely there, he yelled at himself. "No wolves live around here. As for evil spirits," he snorted, "it was just someone's stupid dog, probably barking at some trick-or-treaters."

After a moment to calm down a little, he stepped out of the safety of the tree. Something tapped him on the shoulder. He froze, nearly convinced himself he hadn't felt it, when it tapped him again.

He didn't remember getting to the next tree or how he managed to get five feet off the ground and on the bottom branch. Teeth chattering, he looked back to see a small twig from the last tree waving in the wind.

Now he really got mad at himself. So far, he had let himself get scared by leaves blowing around, a cat, a dog, and a harmless piece of wood. Well, nothing more would send him running. He was going to walk the rest of the way, calmly and with dignity. He'd show those kids, who teased him, that this Ichabod was not going to be scared of anything anymore.

After convincing his hands to release their death grip on the branch, he lowered himself to the ground, brushed a bit of bark from his behind, straightened his clothes, and stepped out. With his head held high, he heard rustling leaves again, the cat's meowing, the dog's howling, saw branches swaying, but his steps never faltered. He took one after another, calmly and slowly.

When he finally made it to the other side, he turned and looked back. That hadn't been so bad. He had made it in one piece. Right there and then, he vowed he would never be afraid to walk past here in the dark again. After all, there was no such thing as ghosts. This wasn't Sleepy Hollow. There was no Headless Horseman. And most of all, his name wasn't Ichabod Crane. He was Mervin Alvin Morgan and he was not afraid.

Then he heard it…a soft clumping sound. The sound of…a horse?

Slowly, he turned. Before him stood a dark figure with a pumpkin for a head, eyes blinking red. From behind the figure stepped a ghost, its shape moving with the wind.

"Ack!" Icky said. He meant to scream, he wanted to scream, he had to scream, but all he could get out was, "Ack!"

Hands appeared, grasped the pumpkin head and slowly began lifting it from the figure's shoulders. "Icky!" it moaned.

Goosebumps warred with icy chills for possession of his body. He didn't wait to see what would happen next. "Ack!"

Too bad no one timed his frantic dash home, two blocks away. He might have been asked to join the track team.

The pumpkin came off to reveal a puzzled face. "Wow! Did you see Icky run?"

The "ghost" lifted his costume as well. "He was really moving! What's the matter with him, anyway?"

The first kid shrugged. "I dunno. Icky's weird. I guess we'll have to find our brother ourselves." He put the pumpkin head back on. "Come on."

The ghost put his costume back down, then lifted its edge back off the ground. His feet clumped in his father's shoes that were too big, as he followed his brother to the next house.

Afterword

By Linda L Taylor
Author of

Icky, Acky Hallowe'en

Why do I write the style I write? The number of things I'm afraid of vastly out number the things I'm not afraid of. I am very capable of scaring myself over nothing at all. I'm not afraid of cemeteries. Except at night. And on Hallowe'en.

I started writing in high school. A few novels and short stories. The first few novels were good only in the sense that I finished them. Other than that, it's best not to talk about them. I stopped in the eighties. I got stuck in that cycle, can't get published without an agent, can't get an agent without publishing.

But I recently met Lynette White and the excitement of getting story ideas down on paper came back. Big time. I plan on polishing a lot more of my existing work. Expect to see more of me.

But, wait! What is that in the dark corner of the room?

Walking in the Dark
By Rebecca Lacy

October 31, 1986

Dear Diary:

Ever since I was a little girl, I've been aware there are nights when the clouds and moon come together to foreshadow doom, warning of an evilness that pervades the darkness. Tonight was such a night.

Everything started off great. I met Jennifer and Suzie at the Roxy to see "Elm Street Zombies IV." Oh my God, it was so scary!!! I thought I would pee my pants, which would have been soooo embarrassing since Eric was there. He is totally cute!!!

In the movie, the prom king and queen leave the party to go for a walk in the woods, which is ridiculous since she was wearing these adorable shoes with like four inch heels. It's a really creepy night, and they are kissing in the shadows when they're attacked by a band of zombies. When they went back into the dance, no one realized they had become zombies until they started slashing everyone. There were gallons of blood everywhere. I kept yelling, 'Watch out!' but those people in movies are so dumb. I mean, really, who goes for a walk in the woods at night?

Anyway, after the movie, Jen and Suzie left before I realized Tina wouldn't start. (I call my car Tina because she's so cute and tiny.) Time after time I turned the key, trying desperately while everyone else drove away, oblivious to my plight. Fear clutched my throat as I remembered the woman in the movie who was eviscerated (this was a vocabulary word last week in Mrs. Shelly's class!!!) in her stalled car. I trembled with a sense of foreboding, but I resolved to stay strong.

I tried the key one more time, furiously pumping the gas, begging Tina to start. When she didn't, I knew I would have to go for help. Leaving the sanctuary of my car, I walked across the parking lot with great trepidation. My blood ran cold as a shadow, which looked a lot like Chupacabra, passed in front of me. I forced myself to keep moving. I knew my best chance for survival was to get help from someone inside the theatre.

When I finally reached the doors, I pounded on them in desperation until my fists were bruised. Alas, it was to no avail - the building was deserted. Spotting a phone booth, I felt a surge of hope that all was not lost. I fumbled for a coin, but I dropped it, and heard it roll away into the gloom. I dug deeper into the corners of my purse, finding one last quarter. I grasped it, knowing it just might be my last hope. With a trembling hand, I deposited it, but the prospect of salvation was met with silence. The telephone was dead and I was left to the mercy of whatever lurked in the shadows.

I walked back to Tina and tried to start her one last time, but it was no use. I knew then the only thing for me to do was to walk home... alone. Dread oozed from my every pore!!!

I walked down Main Street, the sound of my heels echoing off the buildings, alerting all the evil lurking in the darkness to my presence. The streetlights seemed to mock me as though I was prey caught in their crosshairs.

Finally, I turned onto Goreham Road, where I have lived all my life. It's always seemed like a safe, inviting place – that is until tonight. The trees I had never given a thought to lined either side of the road, stretching their long, crooked limbs, taunting me. I shivered at the thought of their dead fingers against my skin and hurried on.

The wind started to blow and something stirred on the Miller's porch. The rattle may have been their bamboo wind chime or it might have been the bones of skeletons struggling to break their bonds with the earth. I had no intention of lingering to find out which it was.

As I continued down the road, clouds passed over the sliver of moon, extinguishing its meager light and my pace quickened as I walked on in the menacing darkness. Soon, I came to the old Mortimer place. I never noticed how scary it is!!! The way the roof has collapsed makes it look as though the whole thing is being sucked into the earth. The jagged edges of broken windows glint in the faint moonlight like the teeth of some hungry monster.

Did you know Ezra Mortimer shot himself right there on the front porch? People still talk about how he went crazy and killed his wife because she burned the biscuits. Then after a few days, he was so lonely without her, he killed himself. They say his ghost sits on the porch every night, waiting for someone to pass by, someone who will keep him company for all eternity. Fearful he might decide to take me as his ghostly child-bride, I tiptoed noiselessly until I got safely past the house, beads of sweat forming on my brow in spite of the cool night air.

Just as I thought I was out of immediate danger, I

realized I still had to pass the family's cemetery plot where the silhouettes of crumbling tombstones taunted me. Near Minerva Mortimer's grave I saw something move. Suddenly the silence of the night was pierced by a scream, which sounded as though she was being murdered all over again. Something flew up into the night sky, casting a hideous shadow across my path. I bolted, even though I couldn't see more than a few feet in front of me.

Finally, I slowed, hoping that I had left the horrors that lie in wait at the Mortimer place far behind. Just then, however, I saw a sight that caused my blood to curdle, and for a moment I thought I would faint. I clung to consciousness, certain if I didn't it would mean my demise. Just ahead of me, hanging over the road, was something so horrible I didn't dare to look at it, yet I was compelled to. It was the body of John Greene, the horse thief who was lynched there more than a hundred years ago. As it twisted in the wind, like a kite caught in a tree, its arms and legs flailed about fighting to be free of the noose. I was certain if I walked too close he would reach out with rotting flesh and grab me and I would be unable to free myself. Tears sprang to my eyes as I selflessly thought of how desolate my poor parents would be. Determined to save myself, I crossed to the other side of the road and ran past the corpse as fast as I could. The sound of John Greene, laughing at my foolish attempt to elude Fate, sounded like the rustle of dry leaves.

I ran until my breath felt like searing daggers in my chest and I could run no more. I was nearly home, and beginning to think I was safe when I became aware of plodding footsteps all around me, slowly encircling me.

Everywhere I turned, I saw dark shapes looming against the backdrop of night. This time there was nowhere to run; no escape from the doom that awaited me. In the grip of terror, I backed away from a creature coming toward me. My heel caught on something and I was thrown to the ground. I nearly swooned as some loathsome fiend licked my face, tasting my fear.

As the clouds parted and the moonlight began to illuminate the road once more, I trembled in anticipation of seeing what horrors surrounded me. It was the zombies! Just like in the movie, they had broken free and were out to exact their revenge on the living. As I awaited the end, I promised myself I would face death as bravely as possible.

The dark shapes slowly took form and I realized they were only Joe Thompson's cows, which had escaped from the field again, and it was his beagle, Burt, who licked my face.

It seems the only horror on the road tonight was my own imagination. How embarrassing!

Goodnight, Dear Diary, and Happy Hallowe'en!

Your friend,

Jessica

AFTERWORD

By Rebecca Lacy
Author of

Walking in the Dark

Walking in the Dark harkens back to the author's childhood when being outside alone at night could make her imagination run wild. At times such as those, hyperbole reigned supreme – making even the mundane appear to be a monster.

Rebecca has been published in several anthologies, and writes a column, Extraordinary Ordinary Women, for www.womensvoicesmagazine.com. She is also the co-author of Leadership in Wonderland, a non-traditional leadership book, and is working on two novels.

Family Hallowe'en Traditions
By Glenda Reynolds

I opened my eyes when my mother entered my bedroom. She looked around to inspect the orderliness of it, or the lack thereof.

"Don't worry, Mom. I'll pick up my clothes when I get out of bed."

My mom turned to look at my pictures, baseball trophies, and various things a twelve-year-old boy would display on a dresser top. Her fingers traced the image of my face as her eyes lingered there.

"You always took after your father, my handsome boy," she said as she sniffed.

"Mom, don't get mushy. It's just a stupid picture for the yearbook."

"Chris, I love you, honey," she said as she put the framed photo back on the dresser.

She turned her gaze to the rest of the room. After wiping her cheek, she closed the door.

"I love you too, Mom," I uttered to myself, breaking the silence in my dark bedroom. As promised, I jumped out of bed to pick up my mess. To my surprise, there weren't any clothes on the floor. In fact, it was immaculate.

How can that be? I'm never this tidy.

My eyes were drawn to the curtains.

Strange, I don't remember those curtains being hung.

I walked into the kitchen and took the bar stool next to my dad. He was finishing his coffee while reading the paper.

"You know, Dad, newspapers are becoming a thing of the past. You need to catch the news on your smart phone. They have apps for that you know."

"Says here, on page 8 of the Herald, that trick-or-treaters are welcome at the mall between 7 p.m. and 9 p.m.," announced my dad.

"Good! Does this mean that we can eat at the Food Court after work?" Mom asked.

"No, I would like to pick up some fast food to bring home. After all, it's tradition for the Ghoul Master, meaning myself, to hand out candy to the trick-or-treaters. I don't see why we have to stop doing that since the accident."

"Okay, go ahead. Make it Chinese," said Mom.

"Burgers, curly fries, and a shake would suit me just fine," I said. But they ignored me. I know, poor choice of food. But hey, it can't be any worse than Hallowe'en candy.

I decided to hit my favorite childhood spots before the evening's festivities got under way.

There was some kind of commotion at the Brown's house, where my friend Susan lived. Her parents were sitting on the porch. Mrs. Brown picked up a perfectly good jack-o-lantern and threw it into the front yard where it broke in pieces. She was shouting and crying at the same time. Mr. Brown wrapped his arms around his wife as they gently swung back and forth. The muffled sounds of her sobs mixed with the creaking of the chain suspended swing.

I spent the day at the lake where I had shot many a can and sank them to the bottom. There at the water's edge was the tree that I carved mine and Susan's initials, outlined with a heart. Someone made a homemade wreath from twigs and red silk flowers; this was nailed to the tree trunk. There were a few notes that said, "I miss you," as well as other sentiments done artistically on notebook paper by my peers.

I strolled the back road along the woods until I came to the Crab Shack. The smell of steamed crabs mixed with Chesapeake Bay seasoning wafted through the air. My walk took me past MacArthur's cornfield and to the baseball diamond where a group of young boys were playing a little softball and the lightening bugs had come out. I loved playing with these bugs and often collected them in a jar. I didn't feel like catching them today.

Still thinking about the lightening bugs, I came to Chuck's Salvage and Towing. The only streetlight on the property shone brightly on a smashed up white Mustang with red stripes stretching the length of the car down the middle of it. The vehicle was grossly twisted, as if it had bent around a large obstacle on impact.

With a grimace, I headed home.

Mom was decorating inside and out with Hallowe'en decorations. At the front door, there was a motion activated box that emitted gruesome laughter and screams. Fake cob webs and rubber spiders hung around the door frame. Small fabricated jack-o-lanterns, with tea candles, sat on the window sills at the front of the house. I went to my bedroom and opened my closet to get my Captain America Hallowe'en costume. That's odd! It was missing, and so were my clothes.

"That's okay. I don't feel like dressing up anyway," I muttered to myself.

Dad was shoveling Chinese food in his mouth in a

hurry. He would soon be busy giving candy out at the door. He wanted to put a little ghoulish ensemble on before Mom put him to work. No doubt he'll dress up like Michael Jackson from the old 1983 "Thriller" video. He does this every year.

I left the house and walked to Susan's. She came walking down the steps as if she were expecting me. Without a word, she slipped her arm in mine as we walked in silence behind some trick-or-treaters. After walking a few blocks, we joined a crowd of kids with a few adults at the corner of an intersection. There were flowers, candles, photos, and letters lining the sidewalk. I saw some of my friends, dressed in their Hallowe'en costumes, holding hands. Others were embracing each other and crying.

Susan and I came closer to the memorial. I bent down to see pictures of myself and Susan.

One of the adults was staring at the pictures and said, "That drunk driver got off too easy after he killed those kids."

"Yes, he should've gotten a longer prison sentence. Those kids didn't deserve to die like that last year. Bless their hearts; their parents still celebrate Hallowe'en after all that's happened."

The adults shook their heads in sympathy. I took Susan by the hand. We looked into each other's sad eyes, unable to shed any tears because the dead don't cry. Still it was comforting to be remembered and loved.

AFTERWORD

By Glenda Reynolds
Author of

Family Hallowe'en Traditions

Family Hallowe'en Traditions was inspired by modern day movies of young people who have died wrongfully and are unable to pass on.

It is a privilege to continue to participate with my fellow writers each month at Writers 750 at Goodreads. You can learn more about me and my published works at http://glenda-reynolds.weebly.com.

Nightmare on Meadowbend Drive
By Mary Ross

Baxter's ears twitched. Had someone called his name? He listened with eyes closed. A car rolled by his yard on Meadowbend Drive. A group of chattering kids skipped past; a clattering sound like kibble bouncing in a metal bowl accompanied them. Intrigued, he opened his eyes and raised his head. He heard the doorbell chime inside the house. Childish voices chanted three words. More kibble was dropped in bags and bowls. He strained to hear the muffled replies of two words.

"Baxter!"

He turned his head towards the voice coming from the other side of the fence.

"Estrellita, is that you?" he asked tentatively.

"*Sí, mi amigo.*"

Baxter stiffly stood up in his crate, on the back porch, and shook his tawny, long-haired body. As he stepped out of his box, he sniffed the warm, moist air that descended with the dusk on this last day in October. By the ache in his joints, he could tell a storm was brewing. He also caught a whiff of the barbecued beef aroma lingering around his supper dish. His nose strayed toward it.

"Baxter, I think she up to something," Estrellita insisted.

"Not the nemesis of the neighborhood." He trotted to the place at the fence where he could see the shadowy shape of a black and white terrier pacing nervously.

"*Sí, la gata negra,*" she said. "Yes, the black cat."

29

Baxter sat on his haunches. "She ought to be called Mavis the Malevolent," he grumbled.

"*No me gustan los gatos*, but SHE give them all a bad...," Estrellita paused.

"Reputation," Baxter supplied. "What have you heard?"

Estrellita settled herself as close to Baxter's bulk as she could, despite the boards between them. Baxter lowered his head, and a gust of cool air tickled his ears.

"Stanley, the squirrel, told me Mavis nearly caught him. He got away, but I saw the big piece she took from his tail," Estrellita began.

"She knows he's my squirrel! No one messes with him, but me!" Baxter growled.

"He also said she made a mess with trash in Yogi's yard. Yogi's *señora* punished him for it. Stanley said he never saw Yogi so angry," she continued.

"That cat is just plain mean," Baxter said and shook his head in disgust.

"I fear she'll do something terrible to Yogi - he's much smaller than she is." Estrellita stood up and began pacing again.

"Yogi's only two years old and just a fluffy Shih Tzu, but he's a fireball." Baxter admired the spunkiness of his other canine neighbor.

"Listen!" Estrellita froze. A light breeze carried the sound of frantic yapping.

"Yogi!" they both yelped in dismay.

"He's in trouble! We must help him," Estrellita exclaimed as she feverishly ran back and forth along the boards separating them.

"How can we get out?" Baxter asked. He stood up and turned to survey his yard.

At the back fence, Baxter noticed the ladder was missing. His master had used it earlier that day to look at the roof. He hadn't returned it, yet. That might be the way to escape, but first he had to get Estrellita into his yard.

"Estrellita, try crawling under the boards over here," he called and loped towards a place where he had recently been digging. His owner had filled the hole with rocks but Baxter moved enough of them aside for Estrellita to slip easily under the fence.

"What now, *amigo*?" she asked while scanning the wall of boards blocking them from the hiking trail behind their yards.

"Do you see that big space under there?" he asked as he led her past a large oak tree towards the back fence. "It's usually blocked by a ladder. My master put flat stones here, but you can see gaps between them."

One slot was big enough for Estrellita to wiggle her way through, but Baxter knew he'd only get his head out. The rest of him was too large. He watched Estrellita inspect the rest of the fence.

"*Amigo*, over here!" she called from a spot two stones down. "The boards here are loose!"

Baxter trotted over and butted his head against the boards. They moved slightly. As he pushed again, a strong gust of wind propelled him from behind. Stupefied, he stared while the boards shuddered, creaked, and snapped from the crossbeam.

"*Amigo*, why are you just standing there?" Estrellita called over her shoulder, "Come!"

"Wait," Baxter gasped, trying to catch up to the fast trotting terrier. Estrellita ran along the hiking trail until it ended at the sidewalk of the main thoroughfare to their neighborhood. Their street, Meadowbend Drive, connected directly to this road.

"Estrellita," he panted when he reached her, "how do we find Yogi now? I haven't heard him barking…"

A tantalizing aroma distracted him. It smelled like the barbecued beef tidbits in gravy he had eaten for supper except it wasn't exactly like beef, but some other kind of meat. He saw Estrellita's nose quivering.

"It's coming from across the road," she said, pointing with her nose. Baxter turned and saw a vacant lot with an abandoned barn. From the corner of his eye, he glimpsed a black streak racing across the street towards the barn.

"Mavis!" Estrellita screamed when she recognized the cat.

"Mavis, stop! We need to talk," Baxter called as the two dogs crossed the road and approached the cat. Mavis flitted back and forth along the edge of a barbed wire fence.

"No time to talk," hissed the cat. "Something fishy is going on in there." She directed her tail at the decrepit barn a few feet inside the fence. Strong fumes of grilling meat venting out of the structure, overpowered Baxter's senses. He shook his head, trying to clear his mind of the intoxicating effects of the scent.

"Where's Yogi? What have you done to him?" Estrellita demanded.

Mavis ignored her and zipped under the fence. Estrellita followed her as lightning flashed across the sky, illuminating the jagged outline of the barn. Shaking with fear, Baxter watched Estrellita nose her way to the barn door while Mavis slunk along the right side of the building.

"He's in there," Estrellita called, "I can hear him whimpering. Come on!"

Baxter willed his legs to move, but they felt disconnected from the rest of him. Another flash of lightning followed by a sharp crack of thunder made him want to whimper. Confronted with an unknown terror inside the barn versus his phobia of thunderstorms, he decided a rickety shelter was better than none at all. He ducked his head and stepped over the bottom wire. A couple more steps and he arrived on the other side of the fence.

"Hurry, *amigo!*" Estrellita urged and darted through a gap between the rotted boards of the door. As Baxter followed the path Estrellita took, he saw a black tail disappearing through a hole in the side of the barn.

When Baxter reached the barn door, he peered through the slot Estrellita had entered. She was just inside the door, staring at a huge fire pit in the center of the floor. Flames gyrated wildly through the grill covering the top of the pit, consuming pieces of charred meat lying there.

"Yogi!" Estrellita yelped when she spotted him, suspended in a net above the fire pit. He wore a muzzle on his nose and mouth and wriggled furiously.

Baxter's heart was in his throat. "Yogi," he croaked, "Keep still! We'll get you down somehow." He hoped he sounded more confident than he felt. When he pushed on the door, it slowly creaked open. He hesitated before resolutely stepping inside.

"Where's Mavis? She put him up there! She can get him down," Estrellita demanded, wildly scanning every dark corner.

Baxter examined the shadows cast by the glowing flames, but he couldn't see the cat. "I don't think Mavis did this," he began but stopped when more lightning illuminated the sky.

Bright sparks flashed through the rifts in the roof. The faint rumbling increased in volume, causing Baxter to cower. Then he saw something that made the hackles on his neck stand straight up. Instinctively, a deep growl ascended from the depths of his bowels.

From the shadows, a familiar figure with a bushy tail, twitching back and forth, strutted towards them. In his left claw, he grasped the end of the rope connected to the net with the agitated Shih Tzu inside.

"Well, well, well," shrieked the crazed squirrel. "What have we here, the dynamic duo?" He cackled.

"Stanley, you did this!" Estrellita wailed. "You lied to me about Mavis."

"You believed me because you hated cats so much," Stanley jeered. "Mavis does have a reputation for being stuck up, but it was easy to convince you she was one bad kitty."

A slight movement to the right caught Baxter's eye. Faintly, he spied a black shape creeping up a fallen beam. The beam rested on the joist from which the net dangled.

"So, how did you fake the big piece Mavis allegedly

took from your tail?" Baxter asked, hoping to keep the maniac talking. He silently signaled Estrellita by moving his eyes upward. He saw her stiffen when she noticed the cat. There might be a chance to rescue their friend.

"It's an optical illusion," the squirrel proudly announced. "I'll show you."

He deftly switched the rope from left to right claw and turned his back on them.

"Now, Mavis!" Baxter yelped as he and Estrellita launched themselves at the squirrel. Stanley released the rope and scurried up a beam leaning against the wall. Meanwhile, Mavis flung herself at the net and grabbed it with her front paws. She and the bundled dog swung past the fire pit, tumbled to the floor and rolled through a large gap in the wall to safety.

Baxter and Estrellita crashed onto the spot where Stanley had been standing. The rotted floor boards crackled and collapsed under their combined weight. At that moment, the fury of the impending storm exploded, throwing bolts of cascading lightning across the sky. A thunderous din resounded all around Baxter's head as he fell and continued to fall.

"Baxter! Baxter!" a familiar voice called in the distance.

Baxter jerked awake, his eyes catching the warm glow of light from the kitchen. The back door was open and his master knelt in front of him, stroking his head.

Baxter stared intently at his master's face. The benevolent features gradually replaced the frightening images of a demented squirrel, a captured Shih Tzu, and the heroism of an uncommon cat in his mind.

"Buddy, you must have been sleeping deeply to still be here in your crate while this storm is raging," his master mused. "Want to come in?"

Baxter immediately stood up and shook his coat. He stepped out of his box, preparing to follow his master into the house. A scuttling noise captured his attention. He turned and saw a familiar brown figure madly dashing for the oak tree in his yard. At its heels was a hissing black cat.

"Go get him, Mavis!" Baxter silently cheered. He resolved to better acquaint himself with the neighborhood nemesis. He thought they might even become friends.

AFTERWORD

By Mary Ross
Author of

Nightmare on Meadowbend Drive

Nightmare on Meadowbend Drive is the first short story I've submitted for publication.

My dog, Baxter, is the inspiration for this story. My husband and I adopted him from friends of ours who couldn't take him with them when they moved to Kenya. I've used his viewpoint in Christmas letters to his former owners to report how he was adjusting to his new family. So, I thought it would be fun for Baxter to have a Hallowe'en adventure to share.

Encounter in the Fog
By Sojourner McConnell

Do be careful out there! I saw something glowing in the fog. I could feel someone watching me; tense, scared, heart beating a mile a minute.

Let me tell you what happened.

Looking back once, then once again, there he was. The watcher was a beautiful, sleek, long-legged black cat. His golden eyes shone brightly and he blinked slowly. He was letting me know he knew I was there.

He looked as if he wanted to see why I had on a pointed black hat and carried a straw broom. He seemed to recognize that we shared a dark secret.

I was not a real witch, but did he realize that?

The way he watched me made me believe that he knew a secret about me.

Why else would he watch so intently?

Did he sense a past that I didn't even realize existed?

Cautiously, I walked closer to him, his back arched slightly. He seemed to have grown larger just in the last few moments.

He wanted something, I could just tell. I was so in tune with this black fearless creature.

My breathing was shallow, as if I could make him disappear with my very breath.

I held out my hand slowly and bent over toward him. His ears twitched slightly. His whiskers crept forward in curiosity. His eyes were wide and glowing as he looked at me. Not blinking now.

My hand slowly inched closer and he touched my fingertips with his cool damp nose.

"Mrow" he said in an almost purr, his tongue rolling the sound into the most exotic word.

I smiled a satisfied smile, recognizing that he had truly found his owner from the past.

That truth had been hidden from me until just this moment. I saw a scene in my mind, as clear as day. A woman sitting alone, in a candle lit cabin, in the dark woods. I also knew that this cat had sat beside the fireplace as the cauldron boiled. The cat and I living together in the steam filled, knotty wood cabin.

I could almost smell the aroma from the steaming pot, causing shivers to run up my spine. The sounds of the deep forest played in my mind like a stereo. Knitting in her lap, dropped in haste at a sound in the dark. Dinner was on a wooden table, that was laid out with tin plates and cups. In the corner of the one room cabin stood a familiar straw broom. Even as I watched, the door flung open and there stood a tall and strong blonde haired man carrying an ax over his shoulder. The woman shrieked! I gasped!

Shaking my head in the cool night air, I realized that this mysterious cat had caused me to illuminate a deeply hidden part of myself. A part I didn't even realize existed deep inside. My soul spoke to him, "What more do you want to share with me?"

Breathlessly I waited for some sign from him. I watched for something, I wasn't exactly sure what. I could feel that there was something he desperately wanted me to know. Was he going to show me more?

He began to move his head. The cat began stretching his neck slowly. He nosed his way into my bag of candy. He wanted to see my treats.

I couldn't help myself, I began to laugh. Here I had convinced myself that this was a creature from somewhere far from here, perhaps even from outer space or from a time long forgotten.

He looked up at me and I saw a twinkle in his left eye. He obviously knew what an effect he had on me. It seemed to have tickled him. He wanted me thirsting for answers.

I smiled and offered him a sample of my candy. He nosed at the treats but would not partake of my treasures. Confused as to what he wanted from me, I started my slow trek home. It was getting late and I was ready to return to my own well lit and secure home.

It was time to call a halt to my evening of begging and threatening. I had not been forced to pass out tricks since everyone had been willing to share their treats with a small witch. I was satisfied with my bag of treasures.

To my surprise he began to walk along beside me. He matched my pace with his own small feet. The golden eyed black cat was staying close to my side.

As I neared home, he slowed and turned away. I had desperately wanted him to follow me home. Deep inside I had hoped that he wanted to live with me. A secret that I had not spoken about to him, but it was a hope nonetheless.

I knew that my mother would argue at first, then she too would forge a bond with him. She would see it was meant to be, that he should become a member of the family.

All these thoughts kept me busy for a while, and as I looked down to him, I found that he was nowhere to be seen.

Did he just disappear?

I looked up and down the dark foggy street. I couldn't see those golden eyes shining anywhere.

I reached my porch and I sat for what seemed like an hour. I hoped that by sitting here long enough, he would walk back into my life. I longed for him to return and beg for candy. I was willing to share with him. We had shared a bond. It was crystal clear in my mind that we were meant to be together. He should be mine.

I sat there growing colder and colder, watching for those glowing eyes. I sat on the steps, with my bag of treats between my knees. I was huddled under the fading glow of the pumpkin that was mocking me with his squinted eyes and toothy grin.

Soon my mother stepped outside to find me.

She said, "It's time to come inside. No more tricks or treats for you!"

I spent the next short while following at her heels, explaining to her the mysterious feelings that the cat had conjured in me.

Mother smiled and listened, but it was obvious that she did not feel the magic of his presence. Her face said she did not feel what I had felt. It said that she did not believe anything magical had happened. I had not told her of my visions. I only spoke of my feelings.

When I climbed the stairs to my room, I felt the emptiness of having lost my new friend.

I slept that night, burrowed under my heavy quilt,

with visions of a life long ago past. Vague memories seemed to float across my mind, teasing me with their obscurity. All I know is that I felt the presence of the cat all that night. I felt him casting a spell over me as I slept.

When I woke, I was unable to grasp the detail and emotions of the night's visions. The dreams that were filled with faraway places and long past times teased me. All day they hovered on the edge of my consciousness, tweaking memories of far away, wispy as high thin clouds. The only thing I knew for certain was that the cat had inspired and stimulated those dreams.

On this, the first day of November, I cannot say for sure, that the past I saw truly was mine. I can only tell you that I still watch for those golden eyes on foggy nights.

I continue to walk slowly in the inky darkness. Slowly, so that when and if a certain ebony cat, with golden eyes, wishes to approach, I will be ready. Always ready for more visions of a life gone, but not quite forgotten.

When I walk at night, I always wear my black pointed hat, just in case. Sure the neighbors point and laugh, I don't mind they don't know about the cat, yet.

I will welcome him with open arms, even if the mysterious cat doesn't return until next Hallowe'en. It will be a welcome reunion, even if his return is only to have a sniff of my candy.

AFTERWORD

By Sojourner McConnell
Author of

Encounter in the Fog

I have had one book published and am preparing for publication of my second novel. "The Shepherds of Donaldson Park" is due out in the summer of 2016.

I hope you enjoyed *Encounter in the Fog* by Sojourner McConnell. If you would like to know more about my works in progress as well as my current and past book reviews, please visit The Page Turner at https://vickgoodwin.wordpress.com.

Purgatory
By Gene Hilgreen

For me, there is nothing better than Northeast Pennsylvania and the change of colors in the fall. There was a time when Long Island was just like it, but not anymore. Builders, chasing the almighty dollar, cut down the trees and try to squeeze another house between the two existing ones. Long Island is becoming Queens and Brooklyn—God forbid. Also, most of the camps are closed during the fall and the vacationers have returned to the warmth of their southern states.

I hadn't been to my cabin in over a year. My wife and I often drove up there every weekend in the past. Those days are long gone—as is my wife. Everything had to fall into place for this trip to happen, and for once in a long time it did.

Hallowe'en was my favorite holiday as a kid and even into my waning years—I still enjoy it, although some kids don't get the hint when I turn off all the lights.

The first part of my trip was uneventful. My son, James, drove, while I read and sipped a homemade triple blend. My daughter was having a Hallowe'en party at her New Jersey home, which was my son's final destination. His girlfriend would drive out later in the evening. I was on my own and planned to head to the forests of Northeast, Pennsylvania for a murder mystery Hallowe'en party, and then to spend the next month at my cabin, finishing my novel.

My son pulled into my daughter's driveway and put

my van in park. "On or off," he said.

"Off," I replied, as my granddaughter Jules, who offered to watch my dog, ran out the front door to greet us.

After a round of hugs and kisses with my two favorite women, my son pulled me in and handed me my keys. "Relax, Dad," he said. "It's only a small bridge."

Perspiration began forming on my forehead and my hands were already clammy. "There's no such thing as a short bridge," I said. "A bridge is a bridge . . . I'll call you." And with that, I got in the van and left.

Not many things scare me. I don't like highways, but I'll deal with them—just not at night—the bright lights bother my vision. I prefer to take country roads and drive at a safe speed. But driving over bridges is my worst fear. I get claustrophobic with an out of body experience—I lose control and feel like I'm falling. My son got me over the Throgs Neck and George Washington—I was fine, but there was a time when I needed Xanax, even if I wasn't driving.

The little bridge my son was talking about crossed the Delaware River. It was only a few hundred feet long and eerie at night—kind of like driving through the Bayou. I like eerie, but it was still a bridge.

I was making great time on my mapped out route, and was finally past the monopoly of signs that announced up to ten different routes this way—with arrows pointing every way but loose. I turned onto Route 209 which would take me straight to the Milford Bridge. My GPS showed my progress and put me at the bridge at 6 p.m., just after dusk. Dusk might as well be midnight in the forest.

Shortly after the sign that stated, "MILFORD 10

MILES", was the turn off for the bridge, but flashing lights and a sign that read BRIDGE CLOSED, stemmed my excitement. I bore to the right, on the twisting road that followed the Delaware. I had taken this route once before, in search of a golf course that I never found. But that was during the day, when I could somewhat see.

Ten miles later the road came to an end, and I had a choice of turning left or right. I chose right expecting to end up in either New York or Pennsylvania, but I also expected to cross the Delaware at some point. The road narrowed to the point that two cars could barely pass and, to my luck, no other car seemed to be on the road.

I slowed down to twenty-five and just missed a family of deer crossing the now pebbled path called a road. I also missed the turn off. I drove over a makeshift bridge, and no—I wasn't scared—just pissed. A half hour later, to quote the great Yogi Berra, 'It was déjà vu all over again'. I waited for the deer to cross and drove over the rickety bridge a second time. Three times a charm I always say. I slowed down to fifteen and saw the turn off to my right—and yes, if I went straight—the deer were forty feet ahead, waiting for me. I must be dreaming.

The difference between driveways and roads—I have learned over the years—is most people pave their driveways. So this barely ten-foot wide pebbled thing I was on was called a road. A hundred feet in, a sign announced "WELCOME TO PURGATORY – POPULATION YOU".

Funny, I thought, as I reached under my seat for my Glock. I just left Hell, so how bad could Purgatory be?

A good fifteen minutes on this road to Purgatory, the

road widened into a parking lot with a two story bed and breakfast—for lack of a non-x-rated adjective. The blinking sign in the window looked like a 'Wheel of Fortune' screen missing the vowels.

"I'd like to buy an 'E', Pat," I said, just to calm my nerves, but I knew the answer—Cold Beer, Warm Food, and Hot Beds. I locked my van, tucked the Glock in the back of my waist, and walked into the bar.

Clad in a Roaring Twenties outfit—right down to the white blouse and arm bands, the bartender twisted his mustache and said. "Welcome to Purgatory, we've been expecting you. What can I get you?"

"Drunk," I said, as I scanned the empty bar and tables. There was no we—only me. "I'll take a Jameson . . . neat."

He must have not heard me, because he started pouring contents from several bottles into a shaker. "How about a Purgatory," he said, and handed me the foaming drink. "It will cure what ails you."

"What the hell," I said, and downed the drink. The room began to spin, or maybe it was me. For the whole trip, all I thought about was my sequel. Ok, let's be real. For the past three months, I've been in a funk. I sit down to write and play games on the computer instead. I needed this trip to write. There is no internet service at my cabin. I use a generator for lights and bare essentials—that's it.

Me and the room stopped spinning and, as I surveyed my surroundings, I found the room packed.

Most of the people were in costumes, but as I looked back and forth from table to table, it hit me—I'm in writer's block hell.

I recognized the members of Baldacci's Camel Club whooping it up, and at the next table, WEB Griffin's Covert Warriors were arguing with Killer McCoy and a group of Marines from his other defunct series, The Corps.

Mich Rapp and Irene Kennedy were alive and well; both were dressed to the nines due to Flynn's editor continuing the series after his death. They were consoling King and Maxwell, who Baldacci gave up on.

In the back corner, a chair crashed into the wall, and above the din of the music, I clearly heard the distinct words — "I'll kill him!"

The group of people dancing moved away from the ruckus and, standing at the pool table looking toward the bar, was Buck Davidssen, Whitecloud, and Priest—three of the toughest characters I ever created.

I turned my attention back to the bartender, who had shed his costume. I was staring into the beady eyes of Jack Mameli, super sniper and the most dangerous character I have ever created. On the wall behind him was a banner that stated: There's no Mystery in this Murder Party.

The two drop-dead gorgeous blondes at the other end of the bar removed their masks.

Oh my God, I thought. What have I done? Not only have I put writing on hold . . . I toyed with killing off Buck.

"Recognize anyone?" Jack said, as he refilled my glass.

I was still staring at the two blondes that could pass for mother and daughter. I pushed the drink away and walked toward the two women.

I was thinking about my opening line when, "Hi, I'm sorry. My name is Buck and I'm a writer," just blurted out. That got their attention.

The older blonde, who fit my character Anna to a T, rattled off a line in Russian. My Russian is so-so, but from the tone of her voice, I could take the meaning to be 'take a hike' or 'screw off'.

The younger blonde giggled and said. "Pretty funny . . . my grandpa's name is Buck." Her eyes turned toward the pool table where the three men were still staring at me.

I turned my attention back to the bartender, who just happened to be holding my drink. "Where the—?" I caught myself, and continued. "Where am I?"

"You are in Character Purgatory, the land where lost and unfinished characters end up, and my name is Jack."

I already knew that, and not because he wore a name tag—I created Jack.

He handed me the drink and added. "I believe you know these two women and the guys at the pool table, too." He gestured with his free hand toward Buck and his group who were making their way toward me. "Maybe you should leave while the getting is good."

He was right; I knew them all, and they certainly did not belong in this place, and neither did I.

I grabbed the drink from Jack and guzzled it. The room spun for a second until I dropped like a puppet losing its strings.

"Is there a doctor in the house?" I heard Jack say with a tilt in his voice.

"That would be us," said Jules, as my eyes closed,

and a smile began to spread across my face.

~ ~ ~

I awoke to a bellow in my ear. "Sir, the bridge is open," said the state trooper. "Have a nice day."

I don't know how I got on the side of the road near the bridge crossing. But I do know that whatever happened last night felt real and I knew what I had to do. I will be at my cabin in twenty minutes and I am going to write until the book is done.

The End

AFTERWORD

By Gene Hilgreen
Author of

Purgatory

The inspiration for *Purgatory* came in my dreams. I went to bed with the main characters of my Jules Spenser series expecting a lot of groveling over which direction I was going. With the guideline for 31 Day of October and Hallowe'en fresh on my mind, my characters took over. I awoke and starting writing. Hope you enjoy the journey.

Furthermore, I cannot say enough about my fellow writers at the Goodreads: Writers 750 Group where I have honed my writing skills and gained long lasting friendships.

You can learn more about me and my published works at http://BadDayPublication.com

Living Sacrifice
By David Russell

Al Bali was the chairman of the Eternal Living Sacrifice Council. He convened a meeting in early October to address the annual observance of Hallowe'en across the continent of North America. The meeting occurred at Heaven's Gate. The Lord of the Universe was present.

"It has come to my attention, and also that of the Lord of the Universe, that He is displeased with the tone Hallowe'en has taken for some time. There are way too many tricks that now exceed the number of treats handed out by the good people. We are going to be living sacrifices this year and turn this observance full circle."

Members of the council used their angelic means to indicate they agreed. They would support the cause. They would fight the forces of Eltanin and darkness.

~ ~ ~

Meantime, Eltanin and Draco were in a meeting with the forces of darkness, to further expand the horror of Hallowe'en.

"This year I want screams from and by the young. Soaped windows and trees covered with toilet paper are child's play," hissed Eltanin. "Car fires, blasts of fireworks, prank phone calls, dispersion of computer viruses, unleashing of epidemics, worldwide nausea and vomiting, arguing, complaining, dismay and disgruntlement is what October 31st must feature."

"I plan to cause mass power outage at 8 p.m. on the

31st," declared Draco.

"Very well. Anything that promotes darkness inside and outside, that is what we are about," stated Eltanin.

"I plan to cause mass nausea around the world," stated Alphard, the solitary one.

~ ~ ~

The Lord of the Universe had assigned Alshain and Altair to the city of Detroit since the 1980s. Their mission, which they gladly accepted, was to cause declension in what was known as "Devil's Night," just prior to the date of Hallowe'en. They had put in place a plan to dispel the urge for participation in this for years. This year, they would be working on a global scale to affect the living sacrifice protocol. Altair and Alshain were in conversation the week before Hallowe'en.

"I think what we need to do is create mental confusion amongst the darkness forces," stated Alshain.

"How do you propose we do that?" inquired Altair.

"We will graduate a sense of frustration and incompetence. Eltanin will blow a circuit," Alshain replied gleefully.

October 31st arrived. The evening before, the living sacrifices were on parade in the sky. The night was clear, stars were bright, and one could almost hear a celestial chorus singing. Al Bali, Beta, Mirach, and Enalmach had thousands of angels each, that presented a glorious light show, honoring the Lord of the Universe.

~ ~ ~

On the evening of Hallowe'en, across North America, the sun refused to fully set.

"What is wrong? All my darkness forces are calling in sick," complained Eltanin to Draco.

"I know. They seem flustered or incapable of our mission. Assuring them they are not alone fails to compute."

"Unleash the sound of thunder," barked Eltanin, "That will scare the young under age 9."

For a couple of hours, thunder was heard across the whole of North America. Yet, fun was not hindered.

At 8 p.m. the power did not go out. Instead, the Higher Power was heard by all to say,"I urge you, be living sacrifices this Hallowe'en and from now on. Treats that contain chocolate and hints of mercy toward one another will be distributed," announced the Lord of the Universe."I have grown weary of inhumanity. Murder, jealousy, abuse of any form will no longer be tolerated. I only want living sacrifices, that better the state of my created world!"

Children across North America smiled as they were handed treats. Hallowe'en was extended until 10 p.m. in most places, instead of ending at 8 p.m.

The next morning, news media reported a safe Hallowe'en had been observed by all. For once, the observance of All Saints Day was compatible, and not in contrast with October 31st.

AFTERWORD

By David Russell
Author of

Living Sacrifice

Since Hallowe'en in western culture tends to focus on the darker elements of life, e.g., tricks, pranks, ghosts, fear and terror, this story is to counter that aspect. It suggests another perhaps more life-giving approach to this occasion.

David Russell is a freelance writer and has been published previously in ezines and anthologies. He is a blogger on matters pertaining to faith, general health, and the life journey. His blog is titled "Grafted In and On The Journey" blogspot.com.

Miss Spook
By Elizabeth Ann Boyles

Two weeks ago, I stepped back from my apartment door and checked the effect of my plastic pumpkin sitting on the floor next to my jaunty, half-priced, twelve-inch straw scarecrow. The pumpkin jutted out of the entrance's indention by a couple of inches. I sighed. Some sue-happy neighbor would probably trip over it. But when I removed the pumpkin, the lone scarecrow looked pathetic. So I gave up on decorating. Hallowe'en would just have to survive without my contribution.

After tucking the plastic pumpkin and scarecrow back into the cupboard, I headed toward the mailboxes on the building's exterior. My birthday is on October 31st, and my mom always timed a "humorous" card and a check to arrive on the Big Day.

Sure enough, the card had made it on time, and she outdid herself this year with a homemade one. A picture of the Wicked Witch of the West, green and ugly, was pasted on the front, and inside was Glinda, Oz's beautiful good witch. Mom had scribbled, "You're bewitching." My smile widened further at seeing the much appreciated $100 check.

Of course, a card and check are not quite the same as a party. As a kid, my birthday parties had been a big deal in the neighborhood. Black paper cats, plastic skeletons, and glossy pale ghosts dangled in the windows. Orange frosting decorated the devil's food cake. No angel food for this holiday. And of course, the two malevolent jack-o-lanterns on our front porch greeted all the guests.

A few kids called Hallowe'en the Devil's day. Once I'd learned Hallowe'en meant "the evening before a holy day," I stood my ground, asserting that October 31 was just as good as any other day if not really better. Admittedly, no one, other than a fellow Hallowe'en baby, said it was better. I probably should have advanced that idea when my friends' mouths were full of birthday cake.

Now having moved to Dallas, my job as a seventh and eighth grade English teacher fills my days 24/7. The unfortunate result—no meaningful relationships in my new hometown yet, particularly not with any eligible guy. I guess we notice things like that more on special days. Not that I expected a party, but I felt a little pang that the card would be the highlight of the day.

Rounding the corner next to the mailboxes, I met a chill wind and zipped my quilted jacket. I hurried to my parking slot to pick up another batch of student notebooks to grade. The assignment for the seventh graders had been to write a poem about anything related to October. I figured a good number would be about Hallowe'en.

Just as I reached my tan Fiat's door, a black paw reached out from the car's underside. I jumped back, then kneeled to peer into the shadows. Two unblinking yellow eyes met mine. The rest of the black cat was nearly invisible.

I couldn't help chuckling. What timing! I should adopt it just to show I didn't believe the old Hallowe'en superstition that black cats were reincarnated criminals. But no way! One cat was more than enough already.

Its paw came out again. I took another look. From what I could tell, it was a scrawny stray. What harm would it do to give it a bowl of milk?

With my arms loaded down with notebooks, I turned to go inside to get the milk. Something rubbed against my ankle. I jumped sideways, then leaned down to shoo the cheeky cat back under the car. It glared at me as though to say that a parking lot was no place for any creature, not even one with nine lives.

"Okay. This is temporary, you know. I have a cat, and believe me, Blinky will not be happy to see you."

My prognostication was on target. The ancient, one-eyed tomcat hissed for a good five minutes from its post on the kitchen chair. Blinky had owned the chair since my mom foisted him on me and paid the pet deposit. My teenage sister had developed an allergy to cat dandruff.

The intruder got the message instantly and maintained a three-foot distance from the fearsome hisser, whose teeth situation made it all hiss and no bite. After the black cat devoured the milk and cat food that I'd slipped by Blinky's line of sight, it hopped up on the sofa next to me. When it began licking its stomach, I dared raise one of its hind legs. A female.

Loud, ingratiating purring started at once as though the cat knew a potential home wouldn't want to face a litter of kittens.

"You are not staying. I'll help you recover, then it's off to the animal shelter if no one I know wants you." In spite of my words, my hand reached out to rub it behind the ears.

I opened the first notebook and read Mary B's poem:

The Spook
The doorbell rang and I opened the door
Before my eyes was a pirate and moor.
A princess, tiger, and Indian chief,
But scariest was a spook under a leaf.

I corrected "moor" to "more," and smiled at the obvious problem Mary had in trying to rhyme "chief." The cat stretched at that moment, sinking its claw into my favorite blue silk pillow. I disengaged the claw and set the cat on the floor. A little too firmly, I might add.

"Maybe Mary should have said 'A princess, a tiger, and a movie star, but the scariest was the spook under the car,'" I told the yellow eyes staring at me. "Your temporary name will be Miss Spook. Lucky for you, I don't believe in your bad-luck reputation. But, let me tell you," I squinted my eyes at Miss Spook, whose tail was now switching, "the last thing I need is a second cat."

~ ~ ~

Temporary is a relative word. Yesterday I took Miss Spook to the nearby Comfort Animal Hospital. Comfort is another relative word, its definition depending entirely on whether you are the animal or the owner. I'd borrowed Blinky's pet carrier, and Miss Spook's wailing yowls broadcast her extreme displeasure.

I actually felt sorry for her and tried my best to reassure her that any discomfort from getting "fixed" would truly be temporary. How had she wormed herself into my affection in just two weeks? And not only that. Unbelievably, Blinky had begun to let Miss Spook take occasional swats at his tail overhanging the edge of the chair without going ballistic.

After the receptionist greeted us and gave me the astronomical estimate of how much it would cost to vaccinate and fix Miss Spook, I found a chair as far from two barking dogs as possible. While murmuring encouraging lies to the cat about how nothing would hurt, I noticed black loafers had moved in front of my chair. I looked up into warm brown eyes.

"Would you like to accompany your cat into the exam room," the young man asked.

I started to give a disclaimer on "your cat," but gave up the useless pretense. "Yes, if that's okay."

"We like to have the owners there for the initial check-up. Calms the animal. I'm Dr. Tom Bradford, one of the associates here. Welcome to our clinic, Ms. Atchwood."

I chirped a thank you, noticing at the same time the absence of a ring on the nice-looking guy's ring finger. After all, I'm only human . . . and single.

"It says here that Miss Spook needs to be spayed. Let me just take a look." After a moment, a sound close to a guffaw disappeared into a cough. "Uh, I believe you may want to rename this cat. Miss Spook is really Mister Spook."

I'm sure my face turned as red as a firecracker. I wasn't born yesterday. I'd known what to look for. "You're kidding" was all I managed to say.

"Cats keep their male appendage tucked away. You wouldn't believe how many people bring in a plump male thinking it's a pregnant female . . . or maybe you would." He grinned.

"Well, this is embarrassing," I said, thankful my voice sounded almost normal. "Mister Spook appeared two weeks ago, actually on Hallowe'en, and I hadn't decided that she . . . er, he, was more treat than trick until a few days ago. At the beginning, I didn't check the cat out carefully . . ." I stopped, figuring my lame explanation would get lamer if I continued.

The vet nodded. "Well, if you still want the spook neutered, we can do that today, give him the rabies vaccination, and observe him overnight. We keep the cats in what we've dubbed the Snooze Zone—away from the noisy dogs that never seem to sleep."

"I suppose that's the responsible thing to do." I petted the cat, thinking he would be even more upset if he understood English.

After Mister Spook endured the rabies vaccination with just a small mew, an assistant took him through a door to the cat area. I couldn't believe the lump in my throat and told myself to get a grip.

The pleasant vet walked me to the counter and picked up another customer's paperwork.

I'd left my debit card at home, so I pulled out my checkbook and driver's license.

"My, your birthday is on Hallowe'en," the accountant remarked, handing back my license.

"Yes, that black cat showed up on Hallowe'en. I guess it was a kind of gift. I'm new in town, and it reminded me of my home, back in Mineola." I wasn't sure why I was rattling on. "My family would've done the same thing I did — shelter a black cat on Hallowe'en to disprove the old superstition."

"Mineola, huh?" Dr. Bradford put down the papers and gave me his full attention. "I'm originally from Quitman and new here, too."

"How about that? We were once neighbors. And I guess we still are," I said with a laugh. I put my checkbook away.

"You know, my half-hour break is supposed to start now." He pointed to the schedule posted behind the accountant. "I wonder if you have time for a quick cup of coffee at the shop down the street. My treat. No trick, although it'd be a good idea to leave through our side door. Neighbors should get acquainted, don't you think?"

"Why, thank you." My heart skipped a beat. "I'd like to hear how you ended up in Dallas. And I know some Quitmanites. Maybe we have mutual friends."

Now it looks like the doc and I will get to know each other even better. After treating me to the most enjoyable peppermint mocha frappuccino I ever drank at record speed, he asked me out for a more leisurely dinner at a great Cajun restaurant for tomorrow evening.

If I believed in luck, I'd say that black cats bring unusually good luck. Anyway, no matter how things turn out with Tom, I think Hallowe'en more than lived up to its noble name. As for the recovering Mister Spook, purring on the blue silk pillow next to me, he seems to agree.

Wait a minute! No, I'm imagining things. I thought I just saw one of his unblinking yellow eyes wink.

Afterword

By Elizabeth Ann Boyles
Author of

Miss Spook

Parts of this story are based on real happenings. My Hallowe'en birthday did result in splendid childhood birthday parties. We actually had a stray black cat show up on Hallowe'en one year, and my mom let him stay just to flout the superstition. My family mistakenly thought another cat was a female and took *him* to the vet to be spayed. Also, Blinky, our ancient, one-eyed cat, watched the world from the chair he owned. The rest of story came to life in my imagination, and I hope lives in yours.

I'm currently writing a historical romance, *Dragonfly Wings*, set in 1859 Japan, and have completed the story's prequel, *The Year of the Barbarian*. You're invited to my website, **Bridges for the Journey**, at elizabethannboyles.com.

Full Moon Madness
By Elaine Faber

Even six weeks after the World Trade Center attack on September 11, 2001, the nation continued to grieve.

Several days ago, the *Sacramento Daily Sun* editor burst into my office. "Clive, pack your bags. You're going to Salem, Massachusetts to cover their Hallowe'en celebration. Let's give the subscribers something else to think about."

He had me at the words, 'pack your bags!' With yet another gut-wrenching editorial in my computer about 341 firemen lost in the Towers, I was up for *anything* to get away from the twenty-four- seven news cycle.

October 31st is big news in Salem. Every year, 250,000 visitors swarm the city to experience haunted houses, costume balls, live music, dances and holiday parades. This year, due to a full moon scheduled on October 31st, the first full moon on that date since 1974, Salem planned even more spectacular events. Apparently, the occurrence of a Hallowe'en full moon happens only four or five times each century! The next one isn't expected for another twenty years—October 31, 2020!

Entering Salem, I was impressed by the witches and goblins, pumpkins and ghouls decorating houses and businesses, much like we decorate for Christmas back home. Witches are big in Salem all year long, due to the history of the Salem Witch Trials, but this year it was especially so, with the full moon phenomenon. Apparently, Salem's city fathers thought the citizenry had grieved 9/11 long enough and should get their minds back onto business as usual. Let the nation mourn if it must. Salem would strike while the moon was full!

Cornstalks lined the streets. Jack-o-lanterns hung from each lamp post. Shopkeepers, decked out in witch, warlock, ghost, and vampire costumes, hawked merchandise. Every shop window displayed witches and cauldrons, spirits and ghouls. Tourists clamored through the town atop horse drawn hay wagons and carts.

I ate lunch at a little diner and delighted in the attentions of a charming waitress with long black hair, sparkling gold eyes, and fluttering lashes. With a glance, Jenny churned up feelings I hardly remembered, being a widow well past middle-aged, and an almost regular church goer.

Imagine my surprise when she handed me a napkin with a message inside. *Meet me outside tonight. 11:25 P.M. Come alone. I must see you.*

I left my lunch half-eaten and stumbled outside to ponder the situation. With her charms, she had the pick of any young man; what could she possibly want with me?

I interviewed shopkeepers and snapped photos of the holiday events that day and well into the evening. Even knowing it was a fool's errand, at 11:15 P.M, I was drawn back to the diner like a moth to a flame.

~ ~ ~

At 11:20 P.M. Jenny wiped down the last table, flipped over the CLOSED sign, and locked the café door. She had nearly given up hope of finding a middle-aged man with silver-white hair and mustache. What were the odds that Clive should walk through the door at the last possible moment to change her destiny?

Jenny wrapped her cape around her shoulders and stepped out the front door. There Clive stood, as she had hoped! She was blessed with a sixth sense about the future, knowing when the phone would ring or a visitor would be at her door. An oppressive spirit had settled on her the morning of September 11th, as she felt something evil on the horizon. She had powers over men, but on this night of nights, with the full moon overhead, on this auspicious date, her fate lay in the hands of this stranger. Without his cooperation, she could not escape the family curse.

"Hello. Thanks so much for coming." Jenny placed her small white hand on Clive's arm, hoping to bend his will to her own needs. "You're the only one who can help me."

"I'm happy to oblige. But, why do you ask a stranger? Don't you have family or friends who could help you?"

Jenny lowered her head, brushing her lashes against her pale face. She allowed her lip to tremble as a tear trickled down her cheek. A white curl tumbled on her forehead, seemingly out of place among her mass of black curls.

"Here, here, now, none of that." Clive brushed Jenny's hair back into place. "I'll help you if I can, my dear. Don't cry." He tipped up her chin and dried her tears with his handkerchief. "Now, give me a smile and tell me all about it."

"I fear you'll think me crazy, Sir, but I swear I speak

the truth." Jenny sat on a bench and began an inexplicable tale.

"I am a descendent of the judge who unjustly hanged Sarah Good as a witch in 1692, right here in Salem. Since Sarah Good's death, the judge's descendants have suffered a terrible curse. Upon the rare occasion, only about four or five times each century, when the full moon is overhead on All-Hollow's Eve, any female descendent between the age of 18 and 29 is in grave danger.

"As the full moon is upon us this night for the first time since 1974, and to avoid the curse, I must find a middle-aged man with long silver-white hair, who resembles the judge who sentenced my poor ancestor, Sarah, to death. Before midnight, a drop of this man's blood must be placed on a particular stone that stands at the edge of town." Jenny's pale lips trembled. "Would you shed a drop of your blood on Sarah's commemorative stone to save me from the curse?"

"What kind of curse, my dear?" Clive raised a perplexed eyebrow.

"It is so terrible, I dare not speak it aloud." Whispering these words, Jenny clung to Clive's shoulder and wept piteously. Would it be enough to convince him to go with her to the stone? And, once there, could she muster the courage to do what she must do to stave off the curse?

~ ~ ~

Clive was speechless. Never had he encountered such a stunning creature that so captivated his heart within minutes of meeting. Never has such a ridiculous tale so captured his imagination. He was inclined to leap from the bench, take her by the hand, and race to the stone in question.

Only with great difficulty, did he pummel his rash impulses into submission, and sit back on the bench, staring up into the starry sky.

The moon hung blood-red over the city, casting an orange glow across the sidewalks, still churning with costumed tourists, jostling and laughing, their joyous songs of nonsense carried into the black sky on the night wind.

The young woman stirred in his arms, her sobs finally ceased. She dashed tears from her cheeks and looked up at him. "You will help me, won't you? I'm so desperate. We only need a teeny-weeny drop of blood, really. I'd be ever so grateful."

If she truly believed her outrageous tale, considering the unusual request, even a gentleman couldn't help wondering, *how grateful*? On the other hand, just exactly how much was a *teeny-weeny* drop of blood and just how crazy was this charming girl?

Clive shivered. A wind rustled the corn husks tied to the lamp posts. A thin cloud crept across the center of the moon, seeming to cut it in half.

Clive glanced at his watch. 11:40 P.M. "Well, let's get on with it. Can we walk to the stone?" He would humor her and see where all this would lead. His hand rested around a small penknife in his pocket. *If a tiny drop of blood is all it takes to satisfy her fantasy and win her gratitude, I can do that.*

The wind whistled overhead as the cemetery loomed into view. Groups of tourists ambled amongst the grave stones. Raucous laughter burst from the direction of Bridget Bishop and Martha Corey's graves, also victims of the 1692 Salem witch trials. One would think it was an amusement park, rather than a cemetery, from the sound of merriment coming from the shadows.

Jenny squealed at the sight of a man dressed as a vampire, looming from the bushes.

Clive put his arm around her shoulder and pulled her close. She was really a dear little thing, and he wanted to calm her fears. Perhaps he'd bring her coffee in bed tomorrow morning…

~ ~ ~

Sarah Good's commemorative stone gleamed in the moonlight.

Jenny ran her fingers over the grooves in the stone forming the letters– *Sarah Good 1653 – 1692*. "Poor thing. I'm so sorry, Sarah. Please forgive my ancestor."

Jenny glanced at her watch. "Are you ready?"

She drew a huge serrated bread knife from her purse. "We don't have much time. I only have two more minutes."

Jenny's beautiful smile, only moments ago holding so much promise, faded, replaced by a fiendish leer. Only his blood splashed across the accursed stone would make her smile now.

~ ~ ~

At the sight of Jenny's wild eyes gleaming in the moonlight, Clive stepped back. The thrill of the lovely lady and moonlight adventure faded, and common sense finally prevailed. Jenny had no intention of settling for a pricked finger and a *drop* of blood. With the knife in her hand, she crept closer and closer, with murder in her eye.

"Hold on, there, young lady." He backed away, glancing left and right. Where had all the costumed tourists gone? The witches and ghosts and even the vampire had disappeared at the first sight of Jenny's knife.

In the distance, the town clock began to strike. Twelve o'clock...the witching hour.

Bong...bong...bong...

The hour that a real witch, if there was such a thing, might easily murder a stranger, to thwart her twisted notion of an imaginary family curse.

Bong...bong...bong...

Clive's dull life suddenly held a great deal more appeal. He wished he was back in New York and had never heard of Salem.

Bong...bong...bong...Bong...bong...

Jenny shrieked and rushed at him, the knife raised.

Paralyzed with fear, Clive put up his hands, closed his eyes, and held his breath, waiting for the death blow.

Bong! Midnight!

Seconds ticked by. Clive ran his hands up and down his chest. "I'm still alive?" He opened his eyes.

Jenny's cape and the bread knife lay on the ground, but... Where was Jenny? She had waited seconds too long to strike and the curse had taken her…but where? How?

Sarah Good's gravestone gleamed in the moonlight. A small black cat hunched beside the stone, her tail whipping around her black toes. A white blaze crept over her nose, across one golden eye, ending beside her ear, in shocking contrast to her long black fur. She stared up at Clive.

"Jenny?" Clive walked closer to the stone. Wasn't it thought that witches could turn into black cats? He'd never believed such tales before, but... He stroked the little cat and peered into her eyes. "Jenny?"

He gasped. Jenny's golden eyes stared back. The curse! It was true. Poor Jenny. "She needed my blood to protect her from the curse. She still needs me."

He would write his 2,000 words newspaper story about Salem, about the haunted houses and the costume ball and the decorations and the Hallowe'en parades. The story would be colorful and, for a few minutes, the newspaper readers might forget about the tragedy that struck our nation low and took almost 3,000 lives on September 11th

He would write about the first Hallowe'en full moon for the last twenty-seven years, but, he would not write about a 300-year-old curse that turned a Salem witch into a little black cat. Who would believe it? Not even his publisher would believe it.

Clive walked back to town with Jenny cradled in his arms. "Don't worry, Jenny. I'll take care of you. I won't abandon you now."

AFTERWORD

By Elaine Faber
Author of

Full Moon Madness

Full Moon Madness - A full moon occurs on Hallowe'en only 4-5 times per century. This phenomenon occurred immediately following the World Trade Center tragedy of 9-11. The event inspired my story, *Full Moon Madness*. Many of my short stories are printed in anthologies. In my opinion, a story isn't a story unless there is a cat…and *Full Moon Madness* is no exception. This short story was previously published in Kings River Life Magazine, a California online magazine with local focus & global appeal, http://KingsRiverLife.com/

If you like this concept, you will enjoy *Black Cat's Legacy*, *Black Cat and the Lethal Lawyer*, and *Black Cat and the Accidental Angel*, where, Thumper, the black cat with his ancestors' memories, helps solve mysteries. My latest humorous mystery is *Mrs. Odboddy - Hometown Patriot*.

Read more about my stories at www.mindcandymysteries.com

~ ~ ~

The Ghosts of Hallowe'en
By Mirta Oliva

Another year... another Hallowe'en... and Johnny was spending idle minutes thinking of how to present a strategic scheme to his pals on how to celebrate the creepy occasion. On the part of Danny, Ted, and Grover, they were also thinking of the best way to win the contest. In a couple of days, the four kids would vote for the best idea, and Johnny was certain he would be the winner.

A cemetery built on the front lawn; ghosts hanging from the trees; a loud speaker blurting out creepy sounds...those were the first three ideas proposed. Now it was up to Johnny to present his plan – the one that placed all four kids away from their homes, in an abandoned house nearby.

"Here is the deal... You know our parents will only go so far, and our decorations will probably be the worst ones on the block, as usual. I have a proposition, something that will make the neighborhood kids fly out of the house."

"All right, what house, Johnny? Not mine for sure," Danny quickly responded. "What do you propose?"

"Not to do what other kids do, of course. At our age, all that stuff is boring. We will do our Hallowe'en trick in someone else's house, the abandoned shack at 101 Old Owl Road. We will carve our own pumpkins, bring along a few packs of candies, plus four artificial mini-candles each, so that they last all evening. Three of you leave at dusk, one at a time at one-minute intervals, leaving your own lit pumpkins on the porch. I will be the last one to arrive, and will do the same. You know the house, the one with some missing windows and broken doors. I will place a "Welcome" sign outside with blinking white lights pointing to the door. The jack-o-lanterns will also serve to invite children and adults in.

"I'll stay about four feet from the entrance. Once you are all inside, I'll invite myself in. I am counting on getting some kids into the house – either out of curiosity or to claim the usual goodies. At that point, we would scare the pumpkin lights out of the unsuspecting visitors."

It was easy for Danny, Ted, and Glover, to favor Johnny's idea. How cool was that? Easier said than done, the three kids unanimously agreed to go for the creepiest of all plans – keeping their own fears to themselves; however, none of them anticipated there could be a good chance that no kids alone, or even with their parents, would traverse the dark road to visit that spooky corner house, the long-abandoned one full of cobwebs.

The day arrived and, right at dusk - without telling anyone, including their respective parents - each kid took the candies, pumpkins and fake candles to old house. Once a nice adobe, it was now in such dilapidated and horrific condition that perhaps the ghosts of Hallowe'en would not dare to come in for a visit… never mind staying overnight.

The decision was not an easy one, but the boys had to do what boys are supposed to do: to get into some kind of trouble once in a while. But this was Hallowe'en night; they had forgotten that many things can happen in such spooky occasion. They were scared but proceeded nonetheless. The house looked very empty, just as they thought it would, and they could not figure out if that was supposed to be a bad thing. The first three guys knocked on the door just in case. Since there was no answer, they turned the door knob around and found no resistance. The squeaky door opened slowly but the kids did not enter right away.

Johnny had stayed a couple of feet from the porch, as the other boys yelled one long "Helloooo," but there was no hello back. So they cautiously entered one by one, a few seconds apart. Once Johnny had entered, the eerie sound of rusted hinges announced the door closing, leaving the boys surrounded by darkness. Johnny froze, but stayed by the door as planned. He didn't expect that spooky coal-black ambiance – further clouded by dust in the air. But boys should not be afraid of the darkness, at least they should not show it. Amidst moments of annoying silence, Johnny could hear sporadic steps and even the vague sound of chairs being shoved away. He was so scared that he couldn't move or talk. Then, seconds or minutes passed without any further noise indicating what he was sure had been a subtle exhibition of paranormal activity. Not a soul or anything moved anymore. The ghosts had finally ended their show!

A few minutes later, Johnny – still standing next to the door - extended his hands around, but the boys were nowhere near him. He moved a couple of steps forward and, again, there was no one there. Feeling no presence inside the house, he proceeded to light up a match. To his surprise, he could not see his pals. He turned around and around and there was no one there but himself. The match flame flickered out slowly and Johnny felt surrounded once more by that frightening darkness.

Very scared now, Johnny murmured, "Danny... Ted... Grover, where are you...?"

There was no answer. Johnny decided to light up another match. It was not easy, because his hands were shaking. The weak light still allowed him to glance throughout the large room where he could only see lots of dusty furniture. His friends were nowhere to be seen, but where could they be? As if he was not scared enough, a cuckoo clock decided to strike seven o'clock... or was something else happening? Whatever it was, the gong strikes and the cuckoo call served to add creepiness to the already terrifying situation. Johnny wondered if someone else might be there – other than his three friends.

"I am not liking this a bit... could we all be in some kind of danger...?" Thought Johnny. "Could aliens have abducted my friends and I will never see them again... or could they possibly have turned into dust, due to a departed soul's curse... or could they have silently ventured inside the house and a vagrant snatched them? If so, why was I spared?

With all those questionable possibilities in mind, Johnny had to decide what to do next. He dreaded to return home without his pals to find that, perhaps, they had not made it home safely. Also, he was not sure that he could easily leave the house the way he came in, but he had to try. By this time he was really scared of having concocted this failed celebration without permission from his parents. For all he knew, witches and ghosts of centuries old dead people were all around him – waiting to strike.

Deciding not stay in this house any longer, Johnny

reached for the knob and – strangely enough – the door opened. He stepped out into the porch as he reached for his pumpkin. He found it odd that only two lit ones were left. As he came down the three uneven steps that separated him from the short path to the sidewalk, he saw one pumpkin light coming from the corner a block away. Johnny was so scared that he decided to walk towards the other end. It didn't matter since the pumpkin light and whoever was behind it quickly gained on him.

Johnny began running as fast as he could, but in the process, his candles fell to the ground. Now it was only him, the darkness, and some lighted being following him. He ran even faster and – looking back one more time - he noticed that the pumpkin light had disappeared. He was shaking and sweating and had to stop for a couple of minutes to recover.

As he continued walking toward his house, Johnny could not help but to keep looking back until he had reached his doorstep. He rushed inside and began heading upstairs to his room. His mother was finishing dinner and asked where had he been... that the Hallowe'en-decorated table was waiting for him. He mumbled something back and quickly grabbed the phone. He had to do something about his friends. He could not abandon them to who knew what horrible predicament. He called Danny's phone number and his mother quickly answered.

"Hi, Johnny... Yes, Danny is here with Ted and Grover, I am ready to serve dinner for all. They told me you were supposed to join us... Won't you?"

"No, thanks, Mrs. Dornes, I'll stay home with my parents for dinner. Mom decorated the table for the occasion, and the food looks great. But please tell my friends that I wish them a very special Hallowe'en evening without some creepy, ghosts holding spooky pumpkin lights chasing them."

"Umm..." Mumbled Mrs. Dornes, sounding confused. "I'll tell them word for word, Johnny."

The Witches of Mount Zacaratz
By Mirta Oliva

Four weeks were left 'till Hallowe'en, and several school pals were already talking about the celebrations, headed by Jesse Roland. The participants were part of a team dedicated to promoting outside activities. On the way home from school, Robert, Jesse's assistant, joined his best friend to discuss their plans for the upcoming event. Among the various items on the agenda, Jesse was to assign "wicked duties" to all, plus he was to take a vote on the different costumes the kids would wear. As for themselves, the two boys had decided to dress as witches - a well-guarded secret since that particular attire was supposed to be an integral part of Jesse's plan.

"Robert, we have to come up with something unique for this Hallowe'en. I chose black outfits since I've been devising a great trick. Now, I have to find a way to make my project work. It's not going to be easy."

Robert nodded, gesturing toward Jesse with one hand."I was thinking that last year we had a boring Hallowe'en – there was nothing different or exciting. Maybe that's the reason our moms don't attend anymore. What did you have in mind?"

"It may sound freaky but don't laugh... it may be doable. What if we could come up with a machine, similar to a water jet pack - the one that can lift people up about 30 feet from the water? Our propulsion unit would be attached to a broom, allowing us to fly away – not too far - but high enough to look as though we disappear in the dark skies... "

"Are you saying, that we'll take off flying on our moms' brooms?"

"Exactly! ... Well, not really," replied Jesse, wearing a silly grin. "We could make a witch broom ourselves, either out of corn husks or twigs. Bear in mind, that for the apparatus itself, we would need my father's help. He would know how to create a jet flying broom, and we would help him after school."

"Fine, talk to your dad and let me know how it goes," Robert insisted, "but do you really think he could come up with such an invention in this short period of time? And would it be safe?"

Jesse shrugged."Good questions. Since my dad is a mechanical engineer, he will certainly be cautious. He wouldn't consider the unit ready unless he had tried it several times."

Robert nodded in agreement and they parted ways.

~ ~ ~

The next day, Wayne, Jesse's father, agreed to work on creating a motorized flying broom. After all, he had racked up over twenty patents and trademarks for his inventions, many of them profitable enough to allow him to quit his engineering job. During the next few days, the kids visited Wayne's workshop after school. The plans for the machine were now finished, and all materials were resting atop the huge working table.

A few days later, Mr. Roland had an update for the children. "I think I was lucky. I created this bullet-type, lightweight apparatus that can be attached to a broomstick. Let me know what you think. If this is what you wanted, I will duplicate it so that you both can have fun riding a witch broom. Your friends will enjoy watching you fly around in circles, not too high, just a lift a few feet off the ground. Dual wings will drop down for you to rest your feet, also allowing the unit to keep its balance. It's a good thing that you guys don't weigh too much."

"Thank you, Dad. This thing is a beauty! I can't wait 'till Hallowe'en," replied a happily surprised Jesse. "Your flying machine will have the kids entertained all evening."

"One thing left to do, when I finish the second unit, is for the three of us to test the motors thoroughly to make sure they won't malfunction or present a hazard to you and others. Since the units run on rechargeable batteries, they should be fairly safe. I will teach you and Robert how to prevent or solve any problems. A single charge will allow you to fly up to four hours, more than enough for the evening show. Since you are in charge, I'll watch from the distance, ready to assist if the units stop working or simply for guidance and protection."

Jesse and Robert nodded, large grins spread across their faces.

Hallowe'en day finally arrived, and Wayne Roland left for the esplanade behind the park followed by Jesse and Robert. They arrived early and began to set up the show around the bonfire. Wayne was carrying the two lanterns and a tool kit. One last time, he warned his son about safely leading the way, making sure that Robert also observed all guidelines to avoid even a minor accident. The boys, wearing their witch costumes, were holding the two motorized brooms. To conceal the motor, and for better visual effect, they had covered the broomsticks with black, small coverlets.

Neither one of the moms were present since they had smaller kids to take care of and because they preferred to stay at home to attend to the children coming for treats. They were not told about the motorized invention for fear that the secret would somehow be divulged. Having no help from his wife or Robert's mother, Wayne had undertaken full responsibility for the event.

The units had been tested several times and they could rise, as expected, a few feet off the ground.

Around the scheduled time, the kids began to arrive, each one bringing lanterns and their own tricks. A bonfire was safely started. The school friends were perplexed when they observed the covered brooms their two friends were holding. One kid approached Jesse, trying to raise the covers.

"Sorry, no can touch," Jesse said, jokingly. "We have a special treat for all, but let's first enjoy Robert's hot chocolate with the candy and marshmallows around the bonfire. Later on, we will have that special show – different from any other you have ever seen."

The evening progressed as planned, each kid performing his own trick. One had brought a red kettle and, for some odd reason, was holding the lid down all the time.

"What have you got in there?" asked Jesse kind of

intrigued.

Bruce, who could not wait to show his well-planned trick, quickly took off the lid. To the kids' surprise, two albino bats began flying around them, provoking fear in everyone. When the bats had finally disappeared, Jesse asked his pal where the bats had come from.

"From the cave at the foot of Mount Zacaratz... that wicked hill the townspeople dislike and avoid," replied Bruce with delight. He was so proud to show his bravery and disdain - not only for the witches, but also for having entered the famous cave no kid would get close to... except him.

"All right, everyone," shouted Jesse, "It is time for Robert and me to begin our best Hallowe'en show ever. Let the show begin!" The final words were followed by the sound of rattles and whistles.

With Jesse's father watching from the distance, the boys moved a few feet away from the dying bonfire. They both mounted the brooms in style, making a formal announcement.

"Each one of you – no exception – will close your eyes. No cheating here. You may open them as soon as you hear the word 'Ready!' And stay back from us!"

A minute later, Jesse was making the expected call. "Ready!"

As Jesse shouted the word that would start the magical show, they took off holding on to the brooms. They circled around the bonfire a few times, causing bewilderment among the incredulous friends. The youngsters were laughing and enjoying Hallowe'en like never before. The magical motorized brooms were a blast, literally!

It had begun raining lightly when Jesse announced they would ride around one final time before packing to go home.

While the two pals were still riding their brooms, a frantic Jesse shouted at two large, flying intruders, waving an arm to keep them at bay.

"What are you doing... go away... you witches!"

The evil creatures were holding on to the kids' brooms, pulling them away - far from the bonfire, the other children, and the astonished Wayne Roland. Jesse's father tried following them, but soon all four disappeared into the night. Mr. Roland returned without the children, quickly reporting what happened to the police. They all waited impatiently for the officers to go after the child snatchers.

"Mr. Roland, they were probably taken to Mount Zacaratz, where the witches live," commented one officer. "We'll begin the search in that direction, stopping at the foot of the small mountain. From there, in order not to provoke the ladies in black, we'll call the boys' names. I'm sure that the witches will release them to prevent us from entering their compound – something we always try not to do. We will have to negotiate with them to avoid a serious conflict. These witches usually stay inside the walled hideaway and rarely do they present a problem in our town. I promise you that we will bring the kids back soon; however, being this late at night, we may have to wait 'till daylight to begin our dealings with these strange people."

In the meantime, Jesse and Robert were ascending

the infamous mountain, pulled by two diabolical beings who called themselves the Witches of Mount Zacaratz. It was scary to think that they were no longer in their quiet village; rather, they had entered what they thought was another world, a dark one indeed. As they reached the top of the mountain, protected by a high stone wall, the heavy doors opened, allowing all four to enter. The boys quickly turned off their machines in an effort to save the batteries for a possible escape.

Jesse and Roland entered the big area, holding their brooms as they walked. The witches took notice of the mechanized flying machines and immediately surrounded the scared boys. They all began to gossip and giggle. It was obvious they were making fun of the boys' attire and of the strange brooms.

"Aha! Are we to believe that you, little nothings dressed as us, are sorcerers of sorts? And you, stupid children, who gave you the idea of messing with the bats in our cave?" inquired one of the Witches of Mount Zacaratz, visibly irate.

Another witch quickly added, "You must then be aware that look-alike witches must do as witches do... hee, hee, hee. Come on, begin stirring this delicious stew of squirrels, bats, rats and snakes we have prepared for you. You'll love it!"

After the sarcastic remarks, the rest of the evil creatures started laughing until tears came out of their eyes. The boys had a hard time looking at the red, bloody tears.

Jesse, scared but determined to escape, whispered to Robert, "We have to find a way out of here, with the help of the brooms. Pay attention to my visual commands, and don't drink the soup."

Robert signaled in agreement but didn't answer for fear of being heard. When they refused the food, the witches became angry and threatened with starving them to death. Soon thereafter, the boys were taken to a hut where they were made to lay on the floor, without blankets. Roaches and rodents visited them all night long, making it hard for them to sleep.

Whenever they poked through holes in the wall, they could observe, assisted by the moon, that some of the witches were leaving the compound while others stayed vigilant all night.

"Robert, if we get out of this place alive, I'll promise my mom that I will keep my room clean at all times."

Disgusted, Robert agreed. "Same here, and I will never be reminded again to make my bed. If our parents were here, they would finish these witches in no time, but how are they going to find us?"

"Be patient. I'll try to come up with a plan by tomorrow. Stay alert at all times; hopefully, at some point, you will hear the "Ready" word. When you do, follow me on your broom. For now, we should keep quiet... we don't want to upset these ugly ladies."

At dawn the next day, the boys were ordered a multitude of duties.

"Clean the floors, wash the dishes, stir the pot, wash our clothes!"

Showing the usual level of witchery cruelty, one of the evil beings commented, "Such cute little helpers you are... you might as well enjoy your stay here, for you'll never go back home!"

Inasmuch as they refused to eat the sorcerers' food, they picked fruit for breakfast off the trees while they were outside cleaning the grounds. Reluctantly, they avoided drinking water out of the rain barrel full of tadpoles.

"How could we ever escape?"

The boys often asked each other the same question, but they saw no way out. The heavy door was kept locked at all times... It would have to be during daylight when most of the black-hooded ladies were asleep. Or could their parents be able to rescue them, helped by the police and the townspeople?

The two boys were still outside cleaning the grounds about eight in the morning when the majority of the witches left for their huts to sleep. Two of the vigilant ladies in black entered the boys' hut, took out the two motorized brooms, and began to push buttons, but the machines would not start. The boys looked at each other, both realizing that this might be their only chance to escape. Instead of an ignition key, their father had created a secret way to turn on the machines. Wasting no time, they joined the witches and, putting up a childish smile, pretended to help them. They fiddled with the buttons for a couple of minutes, shaking their heads to appear upset at their failed attempts. Hiding a satisfied smirk, Jesse mounted his broom first, still working with the buttons, followed by Robert, who also pretended to help.

Once both were in position, Jesse mumbled: "I think I am ready."

The witches thought nothing of it since they were so

desperate to learn how to operate the machines. They wanted to be the ones to show the clan that they could now get easy rides at night using the kids' brooms.

A couple of minutes after purportedly tinkering with the buttons, but trying not to waste the opportunity, Jesse shouted: "Ready!" and off they went.

First, they flew in a circle until they attained enough height. The boys were astonished to see how their brooms flew over the fence and away from the compound, flying very high as the apparatus never did before. Jesse was debating whether it was divine intervention, or perhaps they had enabled a secret button that his dad had hidden on purpose, so that the kids would not fly higher than planned. To their advantage, their captors would not dare to follow them during daylight. Despite their fears, the boys were enjoying the ride.

"Come back you wicked kids! We're going to get you somehow! We'll take you from your own bedrooms in your sleep! Do you realize what you are doing to us? Come back, or we'll end up in the kettle, you nincompoops!" Shouted the two nervous witches to no avail.

"Don't look back," cautioned Jesse, "Let those two wicked women boil in their delicious soup once the others realize that we have escaped!"

"That was funny, Jesse. I can use a good laugh!"

It seemed as though the magical brooms had a mind of their own as they began descending until the boys had reached the bottom of the mountain. Jesse and Robert, after quickly removing their costumes, began walking - each one holding his partially covered broom. The sun helped them find the way into town. Once they reached Main Street, they saw the Chief of Police talking to several officers. They were about to start their search but, instead, they called Jesse's home.

"Mom, this is Jesse. Where is Dad...? Where is Dad...? Where is Dad...?"

"Honey, wake up, you must be having a bad dream. Your dad is at work already."

"Where am I...? Mom... are we at home?"

"Of course, Jesse, you are at home and, if you don't hurry, you will be late for school."

"Oh, Mom, it was a dream then! Now I remember, we had a good time flying around and the kids were mystified with our show. It began to rain and we came home. That's it! The event was a success, the motorized brooms worked well, and we had the best Hallowe'en ever, thanks to Dad! I remember it all. We then sat to watch TV, going to bed really late after eating more cookies dipped in milk."

"Honey, that's what happens when you eat a lot before going to bed," jokingly replied his mom. "So what was your bad dream all about?"

"It is a long story, Mom, and you would be awfully scared as Robert and I were. I think it would be best to tell you when Dad gets home. He'll get a kick out of it. After all, his brooms could only fly two feet high."

"What brooms? Jesse, you are not making sense. Are you feeling all right?"

"Mom, I know what I am talking about, and so will Dad. Just wait until he gets home..."

The Wiccans Had a Plan

By Mirta Oliva

It was Hallowe'en Day
And Charlisse, the Grand Witch
Pretty ugly... and evil-ready
Had put her clan together
For a surprise Parade.

Everyone feared the Wiccans
Though no crime came from them
The neighbors cursed their mayhem...
So the police chased the dickens
Of the intruding flying-vixen.

The media had been clueless
And so was the town proper
About Charlisse's wicked plot
To play a bad trick... or maybe not
On everyone... kids included.

With their faces in green
They really looked mean!
On brooms that could fly
And evil powers to snatch
A child or two... A sure win!

Once a few blocks afar
The kids would be freed

It was only a prank
To repay the bad rap
The sorcerers had received.

With the feared Wiccans might
Ten witches started their flight
But their secret had been robbed
By the police who was told
'Bout the ladies' wicked plot.

As they quietly arrived
At the crowded Main Square
A few guards came around
Chasing Charlisse and her clan
Out of sight, out of town.

The bizarre plans were stopped
No child was snatched after all
So the Wiccans flew back to the land
Where they had come from
Sweating and swearing to never return.

AFTERWORD

By Mirta Oliva
Author of

The Witches of Mount Zacaratz,
The Ghosts of Hallowe'en,
And
The Wiccans had a Plan

Witches are not the writer's favorite people - not that she claims to have come across one. At least not those wearing a black dress and a matching pointed hood. But the author - knowing them very well - immersed herself in this Hallowe'en Celebration tale that delves into how they live, what they are capable of, and their interaction with children; however, the writer would neither intrigue the reader with pointers or disguises, nor reveal whether or not she had played any tricks of her own. Caveat Emptor.

Aside from painting and writing books - four published so far - Oliva loves to write short stories, essays and poems. Inspired by a series of paper bird paintings she had been working on, her first book in full color emerged. Her next endeavor was a love-adoption story about the pains suffered by all parties involved in the adoption process, more so when some characters used deception as a means to cover their own recurring mistakes. A more recent publication compiled a crime mystery as its featured story along with several short stories, a couple of anecdotes injected with drama, and some essays. Right thereafter, another compilation saw the light as well, covering love, abstract, inspirational, motivational, and other miscellaneous poems.

Shigionoth Seekers
By Christene Britton-Jones

Click, clack, clickety clack clack clack..........clickety click click clack clack......

Words were slowly formed and noisily hammered onto the white parchment which was rolled tightly into the trusty old Underwood typewriter. It was one of the few typewriters still left of the many produced in early 1900's and now favored by John in 2016.

John and his friends had convinced themselves for some time that it was no longer safe to type their creative works onto computers since the transmissions – so they thought - were being lost, or distorted mysteriously into the internet somewhere between the writer, the publishers and the final print.

"Best stick to this tried and true method," John thought as his typing stopped briefly, allowing him to rub his red dry eyes as they grew weary and bleary. Then he stretched his arms over-head and arched his stiffened back once more.

He glanced up quickly, thinking he had detected a black shadow flitting through his peripheral vision, but saw nothing. Stretching yet again and yawning sleepily, he absent mindedly scratched the back of his scalp and returned to typing his nearly finished story in time for the publishers and Hallowe'en.

Clickety click click clack clack ...Click, clack, clickety clack clack clack click clack...

There was more movement in the corner. It was a

darkness that shimmied only for a second when he glanced that way. John rubbed his eyes vigorously, cricked his neck to both sides till he had clicked and flexed vertebrae, then proceeded to plod on. He was methodically picking at the keys with two fingers, as fast as he could, trying to keep up with the words pouring through his brain. Getting it all out on paper, he wrote down his new story about the 'Ancient One' some called 'The Bunyip'.

"So ssssleepy ... must finish thisssss...sss," were John's last thoughts. His head slowly sank down upon his chest and then forward to rest on the edge of the table in front of his typewriter. Soothing sleep lulled him instantly to deep REM, his eyelids fluttered closed, and his breathing became slow and shallow.

In a flash, the men in black, the soulless auto-men, were upon him, immediately brandishing their weapons: those deadly looking Black Marker guns. From those guns shone a bright clear light that showed every dust particle hanging in the air along with some green, glowing, swirling tendrils being emitted from John. The men in black swiftly moved their guns over a typewritten pile of papers on the table, over the one sheet in the typewriter, and over John's fingers and hands. With one final circumnavigation, they whipped them around over his skull. The near silent sucking action of all the green, glowing, swirling smoke was complete.

A thin trail of barely discernible greenish smoke was seen lingering around the barrels of both guns as it was rising up the tubes within the barrels. It had started spiraling skyward just before the death dealing collecting shadows snapped it up ... A sharp sound of two clicks closed off the cylinders securely, safety catches were applied.

Tonight this was a harvest, not a kill; they would return another night for more of the same, unless this creative creature offended their master. For once those guns had sapped the juices out of a creative soul's artistic work, it would make it more difficult for them to compose again before their creative juices renewed and flowed readily once again.

Those stealth shadows swished around and went straight back to their master with three kills and seven harvests for one night's work.

Dr Simoisie would be well pleased with both of these death dealing collector's fresh harvests from yet another writer this night. Those poetry spouters and the word ramblers who believed in free speech and freedom of creative expression were the best and purest source of harvesting of the green essence ever found.

This harvest needed to be back into the processing plant within a few hours whilst it was very fresh, for it always decayed within 24hours of uptake.

~ ~ ~

Dr Simiosie glanced up briefly from his notes as his robotic men in black laid down three pieces of skin, each with a black mark in the centre, onto the table before him and nodded.

Three kills.

Eagerly he snatched up the vacuum cylinders from his mindless minions of death's outstretched hands and held them up to the light.

"Nice pure, clear green, boys." It was top grade. "Good stuff," he murmured to himself as he tossed the usual payment to his collectors, who eagerly grasped their minute amount of Shigionoth. They swiftly turned upon their heels and were gone.

"Those arrogant ...

"Goons!

"Demanding Shigionoth as payment from me, their Master. What I find really offensive is them using my glowing gases," Simoisie grumbled on. "All the beauty and bliss should go to the addicted for big dollars." He turned and walked to his factory floor. "It is I, the master gatherer who sells those small vials and edible potions to the wealthy, it is for those who use it instead of Ice or Cocaine to give their body a mind bending rush ... it is called "Shigionoth." That bliss can last for a fairly long time if inhaled sparingly. But the addicted ones tended to use it up all too rapidly by snorting copious quantities and 'go-Shagah' an extended form of 'Ga-Ga'."

Glowing brilliant green globules float suspended in small nose tubes like miniature lava lamps before him. They seemed to pulsate, alive and growing, until shaken vigorously to blend into the fluid before they were inserted and sprayed into nostrils.

"I am their Master I control them all with pleasure, or pain, or death. My Grouse Worms also work well for me and cost nothing to run." The doctor smiled to himself at the thought.

He, the Master mind bender, usually controlled his people with pleasure, but if they displeased him, then the punishment would be deadly... It was not always the easy quick death by those death dealing men in black. Sometimes it was by Grouse Worms feeding on their partially paralyzed bodies, while they writhed in agony, as they gasped for air. It took a long, agonizing time to die this way, but his baby Grouses loved fresh meat and produced better.

The worms had their uses as well, for in his high security factory in the Margotte district, Simiosie had seen to it that their casings were being collected as a base source of protein foods.

"Waste nothing, use everything, it's all money," chuckled Simoisie.

He cleverly designed this new recycled material and molded it with edible glue into textured steaks. These then were colored the appropriate blood red and sold as synthesized steaks for the mass meat market.

"Live meat for the worms and dead meat for the humans. How ironic," he chuckled.

"Ah! And don't forget those annual Hallowe'en products manufactured ... another high priced introduction, a nice little addictive commodity for those who had the where-with-all to buy from me."

"It's all working out extremely well, just as I planned," Simoisie gloated gleefully.

"Hallowe'en is my busiest time of the year."

"Time to distribute Shigionoth to the adults for their parties...after all it is a time to celebrate a good harvest. Gum Balls last year, candy bars this year. Time to give out my candy made from natural organic dried fruit, nuts, and sweet sticky sugar, and of course, they are also protein bars, so add some Grouse Worm casings mixed with drops of liquid Shigionoth to get the teenagers addicted."

"Eat up, kids. Those candy bars are sooooo cool, with lurid bright green streaks mixed through them, right?"

"Plenty of specially made candy bars called "Hallowe'en Mix" made and wrapped in American Hero Figure colored wraps. Just follow their trail and see those kids going Ga-Ga," Simoisie laughed sadistically and gleefully.

"Those kids will do anything to get more of that stuff...more minions and slaves for me, the Master. After all, I have the reputation of having the best Hallowe'en parties, at the best decorated mansion on the hill. ... and of course giving out the best candy in the city right? I have to keep up my quality product reputation. So convenient, having my factory right next to the only mortuary and hospital in the city, I save on transport cost and have complete privacy in the many underground levels that the public doesn't know about."

"Happy Hallowe'en...candies anyone? There is plenty more where that came from."

~ ~ ~

Available each year is a new candy released on 'All

Hallows Eve' and available only 'till the next year when it would be replaced by the newer version that everyone eagerly scrambles for. It is always first released from Dr Simoisie's house as handouts on Hallowe'en (a promotion gimmick that is advertised months before). They all line up each year like "Black Friday" shoppers.

Everyone wants the recipe, of course, and industrial spies hire kids to get the candy, so they could reverse engineer and make it. Unfortunately, they can find nothing in the recipe that would initiate the 'Ga-Ga' sequence. And, none seem able to source that lime green color. It is a bright fluorescent green, a blinding green that was presumed to be a mix of many chemicals. It shows up as the very last ingredient, listed in very small print on the wrappers, saying, "Colored by 'various other chemicals'."

Happy Hallowe'en, Everyone.

AFTERWORD

By Christene Britton-Jones
Author of

Shingionoth Seekers

What inspired me to write this story? A well aimed and overdue kick in the pants after taking a much needed, well intended, sabbatical from writing. And, while I getting my new life on track again after a breakup, ill health, and a close death in the family.

These thoughts have been rolling around in my head for some time about Shigionoth and those that seek it (candy to some of those initiated and in the know). My egocentrical character, Dr Simoisie, dominates the storyline, for he is an ever alert business man who always has to be in control of everyone and everything.

Suspense and Ghost Stories

Stories to make you

shiver and shake

or just to make

you wonder.

Night of Shadows
by Lisa M. Collins

The train shuddered to a stop and Della breathed a sigh. Five towns down since Seattle, maybe she would stay here. Della disembarked quickly and headed through the small lobby. As she stepped into the sunlight on the deck, snow crunched beneath her feet.

The intercom blared, "Welcome to Essex, Montana. Don't forget, if you are not planning to stay overnight, you will need to be back on the train in fifty-five minutes."

Della breathed in a sharp cold blast of glacial air and slowly exhaled as she surveyed the town. It was nice, quaint even.

"This could be a nice place," she thought.

Exploring was one of Della's favorite things. She inherited that spirit of adventure from her late grandmother, Deanna, along with three quarters of a million dollars.

Now Della was looking for a new home. This was an idea bred from Grandma D's journal entries, from her college days at Vassar in Poughkeepsie, New York. She had traveled much of the country by train and had eventually returned to Poughkeepsie to settle. Her journal had mentioned this place, however, and Della was curious about it.

She stepped down onto the sidewalk and hailed the only taxi in Essex, a bright blue SUV with the word "TAXI" stenciled on the side with yellow spray paint.

"Hi ya, where ya headed," the driver asked.

"Izaak Walton Inn."

"Righty-oh. You'll be toasty warm by the fire in a jiff."

Grandma D's journal mentioned the inn as a stop during a road trip west to see her sorority sisters at Berkley. She and her friend, Kimberly, took the train from Chicago in the exact opposite pattern of Della's trip. Since the journal had a vague entry about meeting a man by the fireplace there, Della thought she would visit the inn. Maybe she could discover the reason for the strange note Grandma D had made about shadows in the night.

> *The moment I stepped foot in Essex, I felt welcomed. I was nearly to Berkley, but here felt so warm and friendly. A small town with a wonderfully charming atmosphere. Here at Izaak Walton Inn, beside the massive stone fireplace in the lobby, I met him. The man who would change my life forever. Even though I never saw him again. Only the shadows in the night.*

"Here we are, Miss. I hope you have great stay," the taxi driver said as he pulled Della's bag out of the back.

The inn was out of a Grimm's fairy tale, with wood trimming and multi-sloped roofs. When she entered the lobby, she spotted her reflection in the long mirrors along the wall. The soft glow of the fireplace and the burnt orange rays of the setting sun lit Della's long red hair like it was on fire. She felt as if she had walked back in time.

"Welcome to the Izaak Walton. How may I be of service," greeted the desk clerk, pulling her attention back to the here and now.

"Thanks, I would like room 30, if it's available. My grandmother stayed here once and I would like to stay in the same room if possible."

"Well let me check the book...You're in luck. Here is the key card. All I need is your credit card."

As the desk clerk slid the card, Della looked over at the dining room. It was dimly lit and only a handful of diners were scattered about. Della locked eyes with a man, but quickly looked away. She could sense that he was still looking at her, but she turned away toward the elevator.

Della made her way down the low slung hallway and stopped at room 30. She felt a chill run down her spine as she slid the card in the lock.

Really girl, grow up. You've stayed in hotels by yourself before.

Della threw her bag on the bed and pulled out a basic black dress. It was made of a soft fleece that felt warm against her skin. After refreshing her makeup, she went down to the dining room.

There were a few more people in the lobby, since the bar had opened at eight. Della ordered the house specialty of grilled lamb and mushroom risotto. As the evening ticked away, she began to watch the people in the bar more closely. Some of the men and women began to pair off, a few disappeared, but the others situated themselves around the room in order to take advantage of the fire.

Della ordered a bottle of red wine and had the distinct feeling that she would not be alone for long, but no one joined her. This was not the warm, inviting place that Grandma D had described. Friendly at first, but now she felt out of place. A stranger.

Around midnight, a new group of people entered the bar. Everyone seemed to acknowledge the presence of the three men and two women. Della tried not to stare, but one of the men was so striking. He was exactly how she would have created a man if God had given her divine power for a day. He appeared to be completely oblivious to Della's interest. So after nearly polishing off the bottle by herself, Della carefully rose to go back to her room.

Della made her unsteady way back to the elevator. She reached out to press the button, but a strong male hand pressed it first. Startled, Della looked up into liquid steel eyes.

"You seemed a bit wobbly, so I thought I would see you safely to your room. My family owns the hotel and I would hate for you to get hurt."

"Oh, thank you. My name is Della."

"I'm Nick, Nicholas Stone."

Della flushed and glanced at the floor. It wavered before her eyes.

They entered the elevator and rode up to the third floor in thick silence. Nick placed his hand on the small of Della's back as the exited. Gently, he led her to room 30.

"Would you like to come in?" Della blushed. She had no idea what made her say that. She didn't normally invite strangers into her room. An uncomfortable unease slipped up her spine. This was silly. What harm could there be?

Nick's smile kicked up on one side. "Sure, I'll just check to make sure everything is secure."

Nick slid past Della and went over to the closet and bathroom, turning on lights and checking inside. Then he stepped out onto the balcony. The cool breeze made the sheer curtains float upward like clouds and cooled the room.

Della slipped her grandmother's shawl around her shoulders, accidentally knocking the journal to the ground. It opened to the pages about the Grandma D's stay in Essex. Della picked up the journal.

> *He had steel gray eyes that seemed to pierce my very soul.*

Grandma D must have met one of Nick's family members. Della was reading the description when Nick came up behind her. He had shut and locked the balcony doors and, in Della's alcohol haze, it hadn't registered that she no longer felt the breeze until his hand touched her back again.

"What are you reading, Della?"

Spinning around too quickly for her condition, Della fell into Nick's chest.

"It's…it's just my grandma's journal," Della stuttered. "I thought I would find something here, but… but I didn't."

Nick held Della firmly and carefully took the journal out of her hand, placing it on the dresser. "You seem tired, Della. Perhaps you should go to bed." He stroked her hair. "Good night and sleep peacefully."

After placing a kiss on her forehead, he let her go and left. When the door clicked, locking behind him, Della stripped off her clothes and snuggled into the covers. As the alcohol haze overcame her, and shadows danced in the corner of her eyes, she thought of the last journal entry made in Essex.

> *The night I found myself in his arms was the night the shadows came. I used to be afraid of the dark, now I relish every moment of the night.*

Afterword

By Lisa M. Collins
Author of

Night of Shadows

Some of the earliest books I read were travel stories. I was enamored with travel in all its many forms: boating, trains, planes, cars, even hot air balloons. The journey books, I love the best, were written in the form of journals. Within those pages, I could put myself in the action and "see" the world from fresh eyes. Living in the country, where the nearest town of any size was a thirty-minute drive, I was fascinated with the unknown.

Night of Shadows brings some of the mystery alive. One day, I plan to take the same trip Della made. Who knows what I might find at the last whistle stop?

Evil in Helen
By Terry Turner

October 31, 1989, my friend Eli and I took a trip through northern Georgia, North Carolina and Tennessee along the southern part of the Smoky Mountains. We hoped to do some hiking, sightseeing and camping.

We had arrived in Helen, Georgia, late in the afternoon and were looking for a place to stay the night. I don't remember how we crossed paths in town with a strange little man carrying an old sword, but soon he was telling us that all the motel rooms in and around town were full. He suggested a bed and breakfast that was close by called the Camio House. According to him, it was a great place to get a room for the night.

I took pause at his suggestion at first because of the strangeness of his clothes, the old sword and an odd looking ring he wore that had a black bird or crow engraved on the crest. But then I decided he probably worked for this small town of Helen and filled the role of a tourist guide of sorts. That would explain his costume, for after all, it was Hallowe'en. Also, the founders of Helen, Georgia wanted the place to look like a typical German Bavarian village with roofs of red on every structure. So it seemed to make sense that a character from Medieval times fit right in.

I had never stayed in a bed and breakfast before but always wanted to do so. With our apprehensions satisfied, we decided to give it a go and followed the tourist guide's directions to the house.

Turning off the main highway, we drove down a one

lane dirt road through a sugarcane field to find the old two story house. We were not expecting the bed and breakfast to be in the middle of a cane field. Despite the fact we were having second thoughts about staying there, we decided to at least check it out.

As we got out of my SUV I could see a storm coming across the hills to the West. The clouds were black and ominous, and I heard an eagle shriek a high pitched scream of warning. The winds suddenly whipped up with the distinct scent of rain in the distance.

The bed and breakfast was of the plantation style with a dogtrot through the middle of the first floor and a great porch that stretched the entire length of the house front. Above the roof of the porch were five windows that looked out from the second floor to the front of the house. We both noticed as we were walking up the sidewalk, a curtain in one of the windows upstairs suddenly dropped back into place as we glanced up. This was my first clue that someone was watching us.

The rather long L-shaped sidewalk leading to the front of the house was made of large flagstones which gave off a weird hollow sound when stepped on. Eli mentioned the hollow sound.

I jokingly said, "There are probably former guests buried under the stones".

We both laughed a cautious laugh and continued to the house. A large black bird sitting on the porch railing took flight with a loud cry as we approached and disappeared around the corner of the house.

Traversing the three steps to the porch, we noticed

the dogtrot extending from the front of the house through the middle, providing a view of the backyard. I noticed another large black bird watching us from the far end of the dogtrot and wondered if it was the same bird that we had seen on the front porch.

Dogtrots were common architect in the old South which served to circulate air on those hot summer nights. There was a screen door on each end of the dogtrot, and we were now standing poised ready to knock.

At this point we both looked at each other with an uneasy gaze. Uneasy because, despite the fact that there were three other cars parked in an area to the side of the house, we had yet to see a single person...... except for the feeling that someone had been watching us through the upstairs window as we were approaching the house.

Now for the creepy part. On the porch there were two rocking chairs with a small table between. On the table was a fresh tray of snacks with fruit and two glasses of iced tea and one of the rocking chairs was still rocking as though someone had recently gotten up and left in a hurry. Despite all this, neither of us said a word, and I began knocking. A feeling of panic suddenly descended upon me. A cold blanket of musty air came down from the ceiling of the porch enveloping my head and slowly sank to my feet. The air had an odor one might experience when entering a building with long-closed rooms. My brain was sending out warnings to other parts of my body to get out of this place. Eli must have felt it too because we both agreed with only a glance at each other that this was not where we wanted to stay the night.

Turning to leave, I saw out of the corner of my eye that both rocking chairs were now rocking. I pretended not to notice and kept walking. I tried hard not to run, but I wondered if Eli had noticed the chairs too. Later he indicated he had but didn't want to say anything in an effort to remain calm. When we reached the bottom step, I heard a strange sound coming from one of the upstairs rooms that sounded something like gushing water. Again I ignored it and said nothing.

I could still smell the foul odor as though it had invaded my lungs and refused to leave. In the distance a clap of thunder announced the storm was near, and I could feel the first drops of rain on my arms. As I walked hurriedly to our vehicle, the hackles on the back of my neck were beginning to rise, and soon it felt all too good to be in the car behind locked doors. The drive through the cane didn't take nearly as much time going out as it did driving in, I will admit that much.

Another realization that sent chill bumps down my spine was the police barrier in the shape of a sawhorse sitting just to the side of the road unnoticed when we were driving in. A sign was posted that said, "DO NOT ENTER BY ORDER OF POLICE". And another sign that said, "NO TRESPASSING".

As soon as we were on the main road, I began to look for a place to pull over since I was anxious to talk to Eli about what had just occurred. I wanted to know if he had seen and heard what I had just witnessed. About a quarter of a mile down the road, there was one of those quick-stop places that sold gasoline, drinks and snacks. I pulled in and turned the motor off. Taking a deep breath and seeing the look on Eli's face, I could tell he had something he wanted to say too.

I soon discovered that he had also noticed first the one chair rocking and then, as we were leaving, both chairs rocking, and the strange noise. The only difference in our accounts of the events was the strange noise coming from upstairs as we were leaving which sounded like the barking of a dog to him but gushing water to me. I was taken aback at this fact as the two sounds we heard were completely different.

We wondered why no one came to the door and why we didn't see anyone even though there were obvious signs of activity.

Sarcastically I said, "They were probably out back burying their last guest."

Eli didn't think that was funny.

We sat there saying nothing for a while, both in deep thought, while our heart rates slowly returned to normal. Finally, breaking the silence, I announced I was going inside to get something to drink. Eli indicated he would get something too, but I am pretty sure it was because he didn't want to stay in the car alone.

Entering the door of the business, I noticed an elderly lady behind the counter. She greeted us with a warm smile. I held the door open for two cute little twin girls with blonde hair. One of them carried a big white cat as they left the store laughing and conversing in a foreign language. I then went straight to the cooler and grabbed a sparkling water. When I got to the register, Eli was already there with empty hands which confirmed my suspicion. He came in with me so he wouldn't be left in the car alone. As I was paying for my water, it occurred to me to ask the lady at the counter about the bed and breakfast. I was curious to know if others had reported anything strange about the place.

"Do you mean the old Caym house in the middle of the cane field down the road," she stated as a fact not a question.

"Yes, that is the one," I said.

"Sweetie, someone is playing a trick on you. However, you are not the first to be taken in by the trickster. There have been many over the years. That old house has never been a bed and breakfast. It belonged to some foreigners who immigrated to Georgia from Europe; can't remember which country. It was a family named Caym, a man and wife with twin daughters. They were a strange lot. I was told they isolated themselves from the community, and many rumors of one sort or another were always floating around. One day it was discovered that the entire family had vanished. Poof! Up and gone. The investigators found a tray of fresh food and drinks on the porch and a large black bird that seemed to have taken over the premises. The house sat empty for several years. Then the county took possession of the property for tax reasons and put it up for sale. They sent an adjuster out to place a value on the property, but the adjuster never returned. The police found his car, but no sign of the adjuster. A month later a man and wife, interested in buying the place went there to see if it might suit their needs, but they didn't return either. Their car was found parked with the adjuster's vehicle. Again the police went out to investigate. They searched the house and surrounding properties, but not a sign of human remains were ever found. However, they again reported seeing a large black bird that seemed to be guarding the place. After that the police roped the property off and forbade anyone from entering. That was 38 years ago. Oh, the police continue to investigate and search the grounds from time to time, but the lead investigator died. Over the years folks slowly lost interest and mostly forgot. Recently, a local man has leased the property to grow sugarcane".

By the time she finished, I had chill bumps all over. I was sure the old lady would have noticed that the color had drained from my face, but she was now busy trying to locate her cat she affectionately called Burla. I looked at Eli, and we turned to the door to leave. Just as I pulled the door open, I turned to the old lady and asked if that was the white cat the two little girls were carrying.

She asked "What little girls?"

I replied "The twin little girls that were leaving as we were coming in".

She said, "Sir, you two are the only other people that has been in this store in the last two hours."

In the car I realized I had left my sparkling water on the counter, but I was not about to retrieve it. On the drive back to town, neither of us said much and decided we were not in any mood to hike or camp. A few hours later I dropped Eli off at his apartment in Birmingham and I drove the short distance to my place.

I had been thinking about the name Camio since we left Helen, Georgia. When I arrived home I turned on the computer, did a Google search and found this Web page:

The fifty-third spirit is Camio, or Caym. He is a great governor, and appeareth in the form of the bird called a Thrush at first, but afterwards he putteth on the shape of a man carrying in his hand a sharp sword. He seemeth to answer in burning ashes, or in coals of fire. He is a good disputer. His office is to give unto men the understanding of all birds, lowing of bullocks, barking of dogs, and other creatures; and also of the Voice of the Waters. He giveth true answers of things to come. He was of the order of angels, but now ruleth over 30 legions of spirits infernal. His seal is this, the black bird adorned with a sword.

It has been twenty-seven years since I have visited the hills of northern Georgia. I have had a few nightmare since then and I think about the old plantation house every time I see a crow or a white cat. I often wonder if other visitors to the area have encountered the Evil in Helen.

AFTERWORD

By Terry Turner
Author of

Evil in Helen

This was a true story that happened to me and a friend in 1989. Sometime in the 1990's I wrote this story exactly as I had experienced it without fiction. After I retired in 2006, I began writing a few prose and short stories.

I got this story out in 2011, dusted it off and added some fiction to make it a bit more interesting; although it was a spooky experience without the fiction. Please enjoy.

Keys in the Trunk
by Terry Turner

Had I known a simple walk in the woods would lead to the strange events of that day, I would never have stepped foot on the overgrown trail. You see, it led me to an old abandoned Corvair graveyard. It is a place that still sends shivers down my spine, when I think of that cold March day in 2008.

I looked for old barns to photograph while I drove down a less traveled road in my county. Then I came upon an old abandoned Victorian house. I got out of the car and snapped a few shots of the overgrown, deteriorating structure. As I returned to my car, I happened to notice an old dirt trail, overrun by weeds and brush. For some reason, I was drawn to this trail and decided to walk a little ways to see where it might lead. Pushing back the brush, I headed in. After a hundred feet or so, I didn't see anything interesting and was about to turn around, when an unexpected thought crept into my mind saying...*Keep going, there's a photo op near.*

Being an avid photographer, I didn't want to miss what could be an interesting shot, so I continued forward. While pushing back more brush, I looked at the trail, and it had become wider than I first observed. It then dawned on me that maybe it used to be a road of years gone by. There was a strangeness about this trail. I kept on coming across odd random objects like a hubcap, possibly from an old Chevy vehicle. I started to feel uneasy, and every time I'd think of going back, the road seemed to draw me in.

Up ahead, I saw a mud splattered doll dressed in a tattered red floral print gown, lying next to the trail. The doll was on its stomach with the head raised. Its eyes and mouth were opened, in somewhat of an odd crawling position, and it wore only one black shoe.

"That's kind of creepy," I thought and was about to turn around, but curiosity got the best of me. So, I decided to go to the top of the next hill, with the notion that I'd head back if nothing else was found. However, something else was found...

At the top of the hill, I stopped to take in a beautiful view of a lush valley, just a short distance below. I was about to return to my car, when a gleam of light caught the corner of my eye. I wanted to believe it was nothing, but that weird thought returned, only this time it echoed in my head saying, "There is a photo opportunity down there, go check it out!"

At the bottom of the hill, the trail took an abrupt turn to the right, just behind a thick growth of trees. It was then that I noticed a strange sight. There were several 1960s model Corvairs abandoned there. While walking toward them, I thought, "what are these cars doing here?"

The forest was so dense with plant life, that initially I could only see a few of the cars. As I wandered about, I found more cars hidden behind more trees and brush. A few car parts were also scattered haphazardly on the ground.

There was something strange about the way the cars were arranged, but I couldn't put my finger on it. I ignored that thought and became more concerned with why these cars were left here. And better yet, why were they all

Corvairs? The only thing I could think of was that someone must have been collecting them, but why leave them here in the woods? Again, I wondered about the peculiar arrangement of the cars, yet was unable to figure it out.

Though perplexed, I couldn't resist thinking how cool it would be to retrieve and restore one of these old cars. I pushed that thought aside and took some photographs instead. In the middle of framing my second photo, something dark and fast shot in front of my feet. Startled, I did what could only be considered an "agile Ninja mid-air turn". It was then that I spotted a large rat, which was just as surprised as I was. It stopped briefly, stared, and then scurried away. I had to laugh at my body's response which helped to calm my nerves. Nevertheless, my heart was still racing. I backed away from the car and quickly did a visual sweep of the area for more little surprises, but all seemed quiet. I framed the car again and after a couple of clicks, I was ready to leave…that is, until I noticed the keys.

Someone apparently in their haste had left a set of keys in the trunk lock of one of the vehicles. One key was inserted in the lock with the other hanging on a ring.

Wow, this will make a nice close up!

While taking more photos, I got the feeling someone was quietly watching me and the hairs on the back of my neck began to rise. It was then that I realized I had not seen nor heard any birds since I left the top of the ridge. In fact, the place was unnaturally silent. Even the insects were motionless.

I was about to go when the keys in the trunk caught my eye again. They were swaying back and forth. I tried to make sense of it. The wind was perfectly still and I definitely did not touch the car so what was making the keys move. My body shivered, yet I couldn't take my eyes off those keys hoping they would stop swaying, but they didn't.

Now, I am about to tell you something, which may make you think I am totally crazy...and perhaps I was at that moment. However, in my defense, I don't believe I was in control of my actions...it seemed something unholy was affecting my behavior. For an unknown reason which to this day is unexplainable, I reached down and turned the keys that were still swaying back and forth.

I waited for the trunk to open easily, but it didn't. I turned the key to the right, to the left and then turned it in tandem while pulling up on the trunk, but it still would not open. That is when I heard it; a sound that I will never forget...a raspy, gruff sound, like something from the underworld, and it seemed to be coming from inside the trunk. You'd think I would have let go of the keys and run, but that wasn't the case. Oh, not because I was brave by any means, but because I do not believe I was in control of my faculties. Though my hands trembled, I continued in my effort to open the trunk.

And then it happened...with a sudden pop, the trunk sprang open. For a moment, all I could see was a heavy mist rising out of the trunk, as if the air had been locked away uncirculated for decades. The putrid smell of decay exploded and I had a taste of bitterness in my mouth. Holding back the urge to puke, I quickly scanned the contents of the trunk and to my surprise, it was empty.

As the reality that nothing was there slowly crept

back into my consciousness, I still wondered about the creepy noise I'd heard a moment before. I moved closer to the trunk to give it one last quick scan. The interior of the trunk was unusually clean, not even a spider's web. Then unconsciously, I reached down and turned the keys one more time. And there it was - the eerie sound. Alarmed, I jumped back. As my heart settled down, I let out a chuckle when I realized what caused the loud rasping noise: the inner working of the lock had built up a lot of rust over the years, which created that sound when I turned the key.

Man, this place is definitely giving me the willies. I need to leave now!

When I reached to close the trunk lid, something shiny from the back corner of the trunk caught my eye. I moved closer to inspect. There in the corner, in a neatly arranged pile, was a doll's bracelet, a comb, a black shoe and a couple other things, all belonging to a doll. I thought about the doll I had seen on the trail earlier with only one black shoe and wondered if these items had belonged to that doll at some time in the past. I pushed that thought aside and turned to leave.

As I was heading out, the forest suddenly took on a strong earthy odor. Walking swiftly up the little trail, I couldn't shake the feeling that someone or *something* was watching me. When I reached the top of the hill, I turned to glimpse the place one last time. It wasn't just the dense brush and old Corvairs that I saw this time, but the whole area around the cars seemed dark - too dark for two o'clock in the afternoon and not a cloud in the sky. And now a strange thick fog hung low above the trees.

Weird, I thought.

It was then that I noticed it - the cars were arranged in a very specific order, one that I was unable to see from my previous vantage point. Now it all came together...the cars were arranged in the shape of a skull! I started trembling, but couldn't take my eyes off the sight.

A few of the cars sat next to each other, forming a curved shape, like an open mouth. And some of them had their trunks open, which cast eerie shadows, resembling missing teeth. I also noticed that the hoods of two Covairs were open that resembled hollowed eyes, which seemed to possess an unnatural glow. The fog was now so dense, that it blocked out the sun. A thick gray mist swirled in the middle and seemed to be coming from the mouth of the skull.

Oh Lord, I *guess that's where all the haze came from so quickly?*

I was unable to move at first, wondering if I had unleashed some sort of insidious being when the trunk opened. Not wanting to cause any movements that might draw attention, I slowly raised my camera and fired off a couple of shots before bolting over the hill.

Moving quickly on the trail, I came upon the spot where I last saw the old hubcap, but it was nowhere in sight.

A chill passed through me. *There's no way I'm going to look for it, some things are best left alone.*

The sound of something rustling under the brush kept me moving. When I glanced at where the doll had been, it was gone also.

This is too much! I started running.

I finally reached my car and to my surprise, the hubcap was leaning on the rear bumper of my Ford Escape. Weird as this may sound, it seemed to be waiting for me. The chrome hubcap twinkled a bit, as if it were saying "Welcome back - you made it out alive". As I headed toward my car door, I quickly grabbed the thing and started to fling it into the brush, but at the last second, I decided to pull back and keep it. If nothing else, it will remind me never to return to that dreadful place discovered on that cold March day in 2008.

Unfortunately, the story isn't over. A few days later, a quiet thought entered my brain saying, *I never downloaded my latest photos from the camera.* Without hesitation, I went to my computer, downloaded them and was shocked at what I saw. The last two photos I took of all the Corvairs, which formed a skull shape, weren't there…instead, there were two images of a swirling gray fog which formed the image of a young girl with long hair. I immediately got the chills. Then I noticed she was holding the same doll from the trail, you know, the one with the red floral print dress. My face went ashen and for just a brief moment, I couldn't breathe.

Since then, I've never been quite the same. I tend to get jumpy easily and to snap at my family for no good reason. No matter what I tried, I couldn't push the frightening events of that day out of my mind.

Then it dawned on me, *get rid of the hubcap and delete the photos of the girl.*

I ended up tossing the hubcap in the trash and deleting the photos from my computer. Shortly thereafter, I started to feel calm again, more like myself…that is, until a couple weeks later, when I went out to my car and saw that evil hubcap leaning on the bumper again. Although the day was foggy and the sun was hiding behind dense clouds, the hubcap sparkled a bit as if saying, "Remember me?"

AFTERWORD

By Terry Turner
Author of

Keys in the Trunk

As an amateur photographer I was out one day looking for something interesting to shoot when I came across several 1960s Corvairs which were almost hidden by lots of vegetation. One of the vehicles had a set of keys left in the key lock of the trunk. I posted a photo of those keys on a photo web site along with a description of the image and someone ask if I opened the trunk.

It did not occur to me to open the trunk while I was there taking photos and I did not want to drive all the way back to the site of the cars to open it so I wrote a fictitious story about what happened when the trunk was opened. Many of my photos seem to have stories waiting to be told. Keys in the Trunk is one of those stories. Thank you so much for reading.

The Old Cemetery
by Shae Hamrick

The old cemetery loomed ahead as John Hancock plodded up the stone path, pink daisies and dahlias in hand. Scattered clouds created patches of shadow across the headstones.

" 'Out of the way' is an understatement, John," Nick said, his gaze glancing out across the hills of trees and grass that were dotted with wildflowers, "but it sure is beautiful. And you come every year?"

John nodded. "I promised I would bring flowers on her birthday."

The October air nipped at his arms. Sarah scampered just in front of them, hopping from rock to rock, not seeming to mind the cool at all. John smiled. Sarah was the spitting image of the young Grandma Hancock. A fitting legacy to a wonderful woman.

"Sarah, honey. Don't get too far ahead."

Sarah turned and danced in place. "Can I pick some flowers for Great Gran?"

John glanced toward the rolling hillside. "Sure, but stay in sight."

Sarah ran toward the meadow, stopping here and there to pick flowers.

Nick bumped his arm with an elbow. "She is so much like Hanna."

John nodded and continued up the path to the wrought iron gate. "More than you know. Has me wrapped around her finger all the time."

Skirting several tombstones, John glanced at the names so familiar now after these last seven years. He kneeled at Grandma Ruth's tombstone, cleared away the leaves, and placed fresh flowers in the small holder put up last visit.

"Pretty flouwrs," a deep scratchy voice spoke.

Looking up, John was bowled over by a big collie, licking his face. Laughing and pulling Charley off, John turned to Ole Toby.

"Thanks. I thought something different would be nice this year." He patted Charley and indicated Nick with his other hand. "Nick, this is Toby. A long time friend of the family. He and Charley here have been visiting Grandma since before she passed."

Toby held out his thick, burley hand. "Well, onced a week least. Nice ta meet ya."

Nick shook hands, a bit of surprise on his face melting into a warm grin. "Nice to meet you, Toby. I didn't hear you come up."

Toby shrugged. "Ya, was busy talking, so I didna wanna interrupt. Jon, didna ya bring Sarah?"

John looked toward the fields. "Yes, she was just picking flowers. Now where do you suppose she's gone?"

Toby shook his head, his gaze casting around and his face grim. "No good. Tha's a bad field to be traipsing. Lots of holes from the ole coal mines. Charley. Go fine Sarah."

Charley took off in a dash, barking. Toby ambled after him.

John, his heart ponding against his chest, turned to Nick. "My cell is in the car. Call the sheriff and see if they can send someone."

Nick looked pale. He nodded and turned back to the road.

If anything happened to Sarah...

~ ~ ~

Following in the path Toby left through the grass, John weaved his way with care. The bright sun, from moments before, now hid behind small clouds. Around a bend in the trees, Charley bounced to Toby, then off again to a spot in the field near a single tree. Flowers in red and orange surrounded the area except for one lone spot. John's heart pounded in his ears and his mouth went so dry he nearly choked. Running forward, John almost flew over the ground.

"Ya be fine, lil' one. We gets ya out soon." Toby knelt just back from the edge. He put a hand out. John tried to push past, heat flaring in his face.

"Easy lad. This groun' is no' so strong here. We need rope. Ya stay and I'll tell Nick and them where ya are."

"Thank you," John said as a cold chill swept over him. Toby smiled and headed back with Charley at his heals. John asked Sarah if she was alright, which made her cry. He changed to talking about school and what a great story she would have to tell. Nick and the deputy arrived shortly with a rope. John carried a flashlight as he was lowered into the collapsed tunnel. Sarah grabbed him around the neck, squeezing so tight as to make it hard to breath.

"Easy, Sarah. I have you now. The dark is gone."

"It's not the dark," Sarah said, shaking. "It's that!"

John shined his light where she pointed. There lay a skeleton in wisps of cloth strips, its left leg shattered in two places. John shivered.

"Don't worry. That was just some poor soul who didn't have anyone to find them. You have me."

Nick and the deputy pulled them up. The ground crumbled around the hole several times, nearly plummeting them back to the tunnel floor. John held tight to Sarah, almost as tight as she held him. When they reached the top and scrambled over the edge, John took a long, deep breath.

"Where is Toby," he asked, picking himself up off the ground. "I want to thank him."

The deputy looked puzzled. "Ole Toby? That ole fella that use to visit your grandma? Why, he and Charley haven't been seen for three years. Some say they see his shade up here now and again, but no one ever got close enough to be certain. Most won't even come here no more."

John stared at the hole past him, then looked to Nick and Sarah. Nick's mouth dropped open.

Sarah scrunched up her face and shook her head.

"Must be someone else. He and Charley found me. Charley even came down and comforted me."

Nick sat with a plop on the ground next to the tree. Something crunched.

"Oww!"

His face went whiter as he looked under his hand. The skull of a canine peaked out of the crushed grass, facing toward the hole.

John continued to visit. He never did see Ole Toby or Charley again. A new grave stone he had placed beside his Grandmother's read, "Ole Toby and Charley. Friends unmatched in this life. Rest in Peace."

AFTERWORD

By Shae Hamrick
Author of

The Old Cemetery

The Old Cemetery was inspired by a prompt in the LinkedIn group Writers750. We were to come up with a story about a skeleton, a tombstone, and something impossible. I felt that a story about those things needed a ghost to go with it. Hope you enjoyed my little story. It still makes me cry every time I read it.

It is a privilege to continue to participate with my fellow writers each month at Writers750 at Goodreads. You can learn more about our group by checking us out at Goodreads.com and searching for Writers750.

Finding Grandma Sara
By Lynette White

What the hell was I thinking? No one in their right mind spends Hallowe'en in a haunted house. Especially when it is your own relatives who are haunting the place! Mom's words to me, as she handed over the house keys, were hardly comforting. "It's your funeral, Kira."

My best friend, Angie, had been dating the audio tech from a paranormal group who wanted to spend Hallowe'en in a bona fide haunted house. And, lucky me, they picked mine! After an entire month of listening to Angie's incessant pleading to investigate the family home, I finally caved in and asked my mother for permission.

The team consisted of two camera operators, a medium, the audio tech, the lead investigator, and all the equipment needed for a successful ghost hunt. This required two vehicles, a van and a Suburban. That night, Angie and I were guest investigators. The sun was expected to disappear about an hour after we arrived, to which Dave exclaimed we were right on schedule.

The moment I unlocked the door, Angie took off with Chet to figure out where to set up the three REM Pods and two boom mics. The two camera guys, Dave and Gary, had split up to test the Flir Thermal Cam, Full spectrum cam. They would also seek out the best locations for the two video cameras. The lead investigator, Carol, was barking orders. I couldn't help but wonder if all this noise would either chase off the spooks here, or really make them mad.

Everyone was busy except for the medium, Agnes, who was always everywhere I was, but yet not actively following me. Agnes seemed alright but she amped up my anxiety level. My aversion to her started in the van, where she spent the entire half hour drive sitting crossed legged in the back. At times she would mutter random words, while other times I thought she was asleep.

I was beginning to regret allowing Angie to convince me to leave the van. Noting my uneasiness, Carol kindly offered an explanation. "She is just getting ready for the walk. It is her way to prepare to speak with spirits."

Ok, that didn't ease my apprehension any.

My great grandfather, and his five sons, built this large plantation style home over a hundred years ago. Our family frequently gathered on the land for family picnics by the private lake, hunting game, and harvesting the wide variety of berries. No one entered the house. Ever! The house sat deserted simply because no one could live in it for more than a few months before the spooks chased them off.

In fact, I was so young, the last time I was inside the house, I barely remembered anything about it. Wandering through the mostly empty rooms, I couldn't help but wonder what it looked like when my predecessors lived here. What type of furniture did they have? What color were the curtains? Did they have pictures on the walls or mementos on the dust covered shelves?

The capped vent, in the kitchen wall, halted my tour. Transfixed, I tried to picture what type of stove was first placed there? Considering when the house was built, it was most likely wood. A voice behind me shattered the happy fantasy of my dear great grandmother bustling around this kitchen as she prepared the evening meal for her eight kids.

"You have a deep connection to this place," Agnes observed.

I spun away, unable to meet her intense green eyes. How could she possibly know that? Carol expressly forbade anyone to say anything about me being connected to this house.

The beads of sweat that broke out on my face were not near as distracting as my prickling skin or constricting throat caused by her studying me like I was some kind of freak.

"Excuse me?" I choked.

"You have a deep connection to this place. I know there is at least one spirit here and, tonight, she will speak to the one she knows she can trust."

I had heard stories about the relentless female spirit who terrorized this house. Now this creepy medium was telling me that this she demon was going to reach out to me because she trusted me? How was I supposed to take that? Because, right at that moment, I was thinking I wanted to be anywhere else in the world than in this house!

Gary and Dave suddenly appeared in the kitchen, diverting the attention away from me. Bless them.

"How are the preparations going?" I asked.

"Great, Kira. I think we are about ready to set up the equipment." Dave announced.

Grabbing me by the arm, Gary dragged me down the hall. "You sure there are no hot spots we need to focus on?" he queried in a whisper, nodding toward Agnes. "Sorry, we don't want to tip her off just yet."

Shrugging, I ventured a guess. "I think she already knows." I moved closer to whisper in his ear. "That woman seriously creeps me out."

With that said, I tried to remember something that could help him. I had little to offer.

"Sorry, no one has lived in this house since my Aunt Rachel suddenly moved out, fifteen years ago. If it helps, I have heard stories that the bedroom upstairs, where Grandma Sara slept, was bad." Turning to point down the hall, "oh, and the kitchen. Apparently things are known to fly off of the counters in there."

"Then that is where we will set up the cameras. Thank you, Kira," he said, nearly pushing me back toward Dave and Agnes. "Dave, I have an idea where to set up the cameras. Let's find Carol."

"Can I come with you?"

Thankfully, Gary didn't ignore the pleading expression on my face. Chuckling, he motioned down the hall. "Alright, come on."

~ ~ ~

An hour after sunset, the designated time to start the investigation, the cameras were rolling. The REM pods were set up in the kitchen, bedroom, and living room. The two boom mics were ready to record the slightest sound from either the upstairs hallway, near the bedroom, or the downstairs hallway, between the kitchen and the living room. The good news was, at least we were not stumbling around this big old house in the dark. This group of paranormal investigators used flashlights.

For two hours we wandered from room to room, but the only sounds, activity, or voices, were our own. Gary suggested we all retreat to the van, where Carol was monitoring the "command center".

Agnes was somewhere on the grounds, doing whatever it was Agnes did. That was fine with me. At least she was not following me around like she was waiting for me to start growling, or something else demonic.

Dave, Gary, Chet, and Carol huddled around the three computer monitors in the van. A cold wind started to blow, so Angie and I decided to retreat to the Suburban. I jumped into the passenger seat, while Angie climbed into the driver's side and started the engine. Before long I let the quiet hum of the heater, and the comfort of the seat warmer, carry me away to the other option I had tonight. I could be at a Hallowe'en costume party with Craig. But nooooo, I chose to be here with Angie, hunting for my dead relatives. I was such an idiot!

The uncomfortable silence must have bothered Angie. She shifted in her seat.

"Isn't this fun, Kira? I am so excited to be doing an investigation at someone's house I know."

Having disrupted my perfect Craig fantasy irritated me, and I slowly opened my eyes, admittedly dramatizing my sigh a bit.

"Too bad for you, then, that it appears the spooks in this house have checked out for the night."

"Not necessarily. Chet says that the key to these

investigations is patience."

A disturbance by the van drew our attention. Gary, Dave, and Chet were rushing toward us. Angie pointed at them as if they were responding to her prompt and jumped out of the Suburban.

"Great," I moaned as I reluctantly followed.

Gary was nearly bouncing with excitement. "Looks like the spirits have finally stirred. In the last ten minutes, both the upstairs and downstairs boom mics have picked up sounds."

"The REM pod upstairs has gone off twice in five minutes," Chet chimed in.

Dave pointed at me. "Carol has a great idea. She wants you to go into your grandmother's room alone to see if she will talk to you through this." In his hand was a small box shaped device.

I instantly covered my ears as the static noise burst from the device in his hand. They were all clearly amused by my reaction. I cautiously lowered my hands.

"What the hell is that thing?"

With a smug smile, Dave turned it off before proceeding to explain. "It is called a spirit box. It scans hundreds of frequencies and the ghosts can use it to speak to us."

"How can they speak over that horrendous static?"

"It is a pretty technical, but basically the ghosts use these frequencies to speak to us. The only thing better is the Ovilus. That is going to be our next investment.".

A movement in the nearby bushes halted the conversation. The face of the figure approaching us was obscured by the coat collar protecting her from the bitter wind. I slowly released my breath as the figure joined us and lowered her collar. It was only Agnes.

"Perfect timing, Agnes. The house has come alive. We are sending Kira in to try and communicate with them," Dave announced.

Was I the only one who was seeing the troubled expression on the medium's face? This was doing little to boost my desire to go back into that house, much less alone.

"Agnes, what's wrong?"

Cocking her head towards me she glared at her teammates.

"I want to know why you all decided not to tell me she is so connected to this place?" She didn't wait for an answer. "I encountered three spirits on my walk. One of them concerned me enough to warn you that, if you send her in there alone, it could go very badly for her. This spirit has a story that she needs to tell someone. The reason she is so violent is because she is frustrated that no one is helping her. I have an idea what is going on here, but I suspect she is hoping Kira will listen. Therefore, if you are sending her into that house, then I am going with her."

Suddenly, I wasn't sure if Agnes was my new best friend or worst enemy.

"What do you mean the spirit has a story to tell? Who is this spirit?" I could hear myself asking.

"All I know for certain is that her name is Sara and she is not only tied to this house, but to you." She started to explain, but her mouth snapped shut as I suddenly fell against the side of the Suburban.

My legs couldn't seem to bear my weight and my hand moved to my lips to cover the scream trying to escape. Dave quickly wrapped an arm around my waist to keep me upright.

Several heartbeats passed before I slowly lowered my hand. "S...Sara," I stuttered. "That is grandma's name. She disappeared fifty-two years ago tonight. Grandpa said she ran away, but there has always been suspicions that..." My voice trailed off as I couldn't bring myself to say that he murdered her.

"Grandpa ended up in prison six months after grandma vanished, but not because of what he did to her." I was too overcome with emotion to go on, so Angie jumped in to relate my family's deepest tragedy.

"He was arrested for physically abusing the boys and sexually assaulting the oldest daughter Martha, who was fourteen at the time. He was murdered in that prison, a few months after he arrived. The five children were split up for several years before they found each other again. Kira's mother was only two when her mother vanished."

"Dear God." Dave muttered, eyes wide in disbelief. The rest were shaking their heads in unison.

"It might be best if you stay out here, Kira." Chet offered.

"No!" Agnes cut across him. "She needs to do this, just not alone."

Determined that I would decide what I would, or wouldn't do, I pushed myself up straight. "Why do I have to do it? You said yourself that if I go in there it will go badly for me."

Agnes, didn't even blink. "No, I said if you went in there alone it could go badly for you," she corrected me.

Dave huffed in frustration. "Can we do this already? Our window of opportunity is closing here."

Carol finally stepped in. "Look Kira, if you are not comfortable with this you can stay out here and Chet and Dave can do it."

It irritated me to see Agnes raise her right eyebrow in anticipation. My bristling pride renewed my strength. I would prove to Agnes that I could handle whatever my dead grandmother had in store for me.

"No, I will go. Give me that spirit box, thingy, Dave."

He turned it on and obediently handed it to me. Angie retrieved the flashlight from the front seat. Steeling my nerves, I grabbed the flashlight and marched inside. Before my common sense could rob me of my courage, I went straight to my grandmother's bedroom and plopped down, cross-legged, in the center of the floor.

"Alright, so now what do I do?"

Agnes sat down beside me and handed me a laminated sheet of questions.

"Place your hand over the spirit box and read the questions. After each question raise your hand and pause for a moment to allow the spirit to answer."

"Fine." I read off the first question. "Who is here?" Then the second "What is your name?"

"Sara," a faint, but distinct, voice came from the spirit box.

Startled to actually get an answer, I nearly tossed the

box onto the floor. My heart was racing, sweat was pouring down my face, and I trembled uncontrollably. My mind was screaming this wasn't real.

"Sara, we want to help you pass over. Please tell us what we need to do to do that?" Agnes calmly said.

The voice coming from the spirit box was nearly frantic. "Help me!"

My eyes were drawn to the corner of the room nearest to me. Standing there was a woman. Before I could alert Agnes, the woman rushed me. The force of her impact snapped my head back. I didn't understand what was happening, but I knew this much- I was not alone in my body!

I was still in this room, but I was standing beside a large wooden dresser. I was furious and wanted nothing more than to make him pay for this. Now, I was outside by an old pickup. I needed to go somewhere to think, but I couldn't leave the children alone with him. Without warning there was an unbearable pain in my head. Just as suddenly as the pain hit me, it was gone, and I was confused. What just happened? Why was I suddenly by the rock? No, I was under the rock. That sick bastard! Our children play on this rock.

"Kira, Kira. Come on Kira, talk to me. Guys, get up here! She's been jumped!" I could hear Agnes yelling but I was so overcome with sadness, and hopelessness, that I began to weep bitterly.

Next thing I knew, I was coughing. My vision cleared and... wait? How did I end up in the van, and why was Agnes waiving that burning sage in front of my face?

My immediate reaction was to jerk back away from her.

Angie's face suddenly appeared in my field of vision. "Kira, are you alright? Dear God, woman, you scared me half to death."

Still unable to comprehend what just happened, I focused on what I did know.

"I'm certain now that grandpa murdered grandma, and I am pretty sure she is buried under the jumping rock down at the lake." I tried to move but I was too weak. Leaning heavily against the wall, I pleaded her case. "We have to go find her. She just wants justice and peace."

"I promise," Dave vowed, "we will bring some equipment out and we will find her. When we do, we will take the steps necessary to help her move on and have peace. But right now we need to take care of you. Being jumped is rough on the toughest investigator. "

~ ~ ~

The team kept their promise. One week later we returned to the farm with metal detectors and ground penetrating radar. We located her grave in less than an hour. As soon as we found the first bones, we called the sheriff, who called the county coroner. They arrived about the same time as my mother and Aunt Martha. My aunt burst into tears when she saw the gold locket resting against the skeleton's sternum. She identified it as the necklace her mother wore, but the body was still taken to the morgue for positive ID.

Grandma's remains have been laid to rest in the

family cemetery, and every Saturday I place fresh flowers next to her glistening new marble headstone. I know she has finally moved on and is at peace.

After our wedding, and with my family's blessing, Craig and I moved into the house great grandpa built. The money we had saved, and a generous grant from my Uncle Bill, paid for repairs and furnishings. The thirty-minute drive to and from work is worth the sacrifice for the peace we enjoy here.

Afterword

By Lynette White
Author of

Finding Grandma Sarah

Having had experiences with ghosts, I am fascinated with the paranormal. However, writing a paranormal story proved to be an adventure in itself. I had to really get into Kira's head to discover how she would feel, what she would fear, and how she would react to being in that house.

When I started writing, I just assumed I would be writing full length novels. That is until I came across the 750 Writer's group. I have come to love the challenge of creating an entire story in 1000 words or less. Gratefully we've been given 3000 words for this submission.

Along with this story, I will be releasing book two of the Destiny Series summer 2016. You can find links to all of my books on http://www.whitefantasybooks.net/.

You can also find me on Twitter: @Lynettekwhite or Facebook: https://www.facebook.com/White-Fantasy-Author-Lynette-White-148573078549707/

Curse of the Incan Mummies
By Glenda Reynolds

Carl watched as the old man beside him stroked his white beard over and over again. The younger man inched further toward the isle to distance himself from the horrible stench the older man emitted.

The plane was nearly full. When passengers stopped boarding, the old man immediately asked a stewardess, "Miss, could I please have a Jack and Coke. Make it 3 bottles please."

Carl snickered, "You're not wasting time getting plastered, are you? Afraid of flying?"

"Not at all. It's what I've just been through that has me frightened to the core."

The stewardess returned with a plastic cup of Coke and 3 miniature bottles of Jack Daniels. With a shaky hand, the old man ignored the soft drink as he twisted the cap off of the liquor and drained it dry.

"I'm Doctor Ollie Banner, by the way," he said as he extended his hand in greeting.

"Pleased to meet you. I'm Carl Hopkins. Tell me, what happened to shake you up so?" He thought perhaps he should have a drink too. He'd rather smell liquor than the stench that the doctor wore. He would request a drink when the stewardess came around again.

Dr. Banner started his tale from the beginning about his archaeological excavation of the Inca ruins in Peru. Soon the effects of the whiskey kicked in, calming his voice and slowing his ramble.

"So there I was, on a bar stool in a Peruvian pub. I was deep in thought about the Incan Emperor Chanti, for it was this emperor who thought his powers were not limited to space and time. He became a legend among his people when he conquered his enemy and stole the mummified bodies of their dead kings. He would then parade the stolen mummies through the streets of the conquered cities."

Carl was fascinated. He had always admired the adventures of archeologists like the good doctor.

"I left the pub and began my search for Chanti. It led me to a burial site of his heirs. After speaking with some Spanish priests about sacrificial rituals, I was led to the highest burial mountain in the world. To my dismay, the body of Chanti and his heirs were not among these mummies. No, I wanted to find where people of royalty were buried.

Further inland, my team of anthropologists and I discovered the ancient Palacio del Sol that housed virgin princesses and priestesses. During our dig, we found two unique mummies: one was the priestess of Chanti whose name was Alisya and her illegitimate son Cezar. Chanti took Alisya as a lover. He figured that this may gain him an advantage in battle with the power of the sun god behind him. When Alisya became pregnant with his baby, he forced her to sacrifice him to the Incan sun god when the child had reached eight years old. Alisya spelled her little boy with forbidden magic that he could be raised from the dead and rule in the stead of his father. After Cezar was sacrificed, Alisya was filled with much grief and rage."

Carl smirked at the mention of a boy raised from the

dead, but this was entertaining. It would be a long plane ride after all.

"Alisya implored the gods to rain judgment on her lover after he went into battle. It was said that the skies above grew stormy. A bolt of lightning struck Chanti in the chest, and he fell dead in the heat of battle. Chanti's army was defeated. This may have been the beginning of the end for the Incan empire."

"This is all interesting, but where is the part that got you so rattled?" inquired Carl.

"I was just getting to that," Ollie replied, looking agitated at being interrupted. "I was filled with delight at having made such a discovery. Suddenly, my joy was cut short when the earth shook violently. It started as a small vibration but built in intensity. I grabbed the little mummy of Cezar and other paraphernalia at the site and threw them with the rest of my things in a small trunk I carried. The remains of Alisya would have to wait.

Once we cleared *Palacio del Sol*, the local anthropologists - who were very steeped in traditional folklore - looked panic stricken when they discovered what I had done.

'*Senior* Banner, you have to take him back! Do you not know that it is forbidden to remove the mummies from this place?'

'Why would it hurt to remove a find like this? It could be given to a great museum for the world to see.'

'No, *Senior*. The legend says that if you remove any sacred mummies from their resting place, many bad things will happen to the one who took them.'

'Hogwash!' I held up my finger. 'One: It is unsafe to go back in there, and,' I held up two fingers, 'Two: I am not parting with this mummy.'

'Okay, *Senior*, have it your way. But just remember that I warned you. Do not blame me for what happens.'

'I stand warned!' I retorted.

The earth shook again. When everything became still, snakes slithered out from under rocks and through their burrows. They appeared to be slithering right for me, drawn as it were to the contents of the trunk. A coral snake got very close. A green viper had already started sizing me up at my feet; its tongue flicked out to smell me. I picked up the trunk and trailed after the other men.

The men jumped in the jeep and started it up. The vehicle took off. I threw the trunk in the back while I was still running. I barely managed to hop in. We drove to the nearest town. The jeep came to an abrupt stop

The driver turned and spat the words out, 'You are cursed now! Get out! I will not be a party to this.'

The other men nodded in agreement and glared at me. I took the trunk and stepped out on the road. They had just disappeared from sight when a storm blew in. The clouds were dark and menacing. Several condors glided on the breezes. They converged on me and rained poop all over me. I was covered head to toe in bird stink."

Carl glanced at the old man and sniffed slightly. He thought he might just be smelling bird poop alright. He inched a little further away.

" 'This is just a coincidence', I told myself," the doctor continued right along. "I saw lightning strike the hotel where I was staying. A fire blazed in the building. As it turned out, it started in my room. I rushed up the stairs, flung open the door, only to see my belongings turned to ash, I tried to assure myself that at least I had my passport and my wallet with me.

I went out to call a taxi to take me to the airport. As I stood at the side of the road in the rain, a young boy ran behind me and lifted my wallet and passport from my back pockets.

'Somebody stop that thief!' I yelled. No one paid attention to me.

Without warning a flash-flood covered the road. It gathered in strength and headed right for me. I ran until I was caught in the waters and was swept off my feet. The raging flood carried me over the edge of the road, down the side of the mountain, where I collided with thick green vegetation. When I finally came to rest at the bottom, I was a sorry sight, with greenery, mud, and bird poop covering every inch of me. Then, a large branch that had trailed behind me, hit me in the head. I became unconscious.

When I came to, I was in a medical clinic - a very rundown one. A note was on a chair beside my bed said that the trunk had been shipped off to the states to my son and his family.

I raised myself to sit. There was a nurse in a chair with her back to me.

'Ma'am, I need to be on my way. What do I owe you?'

The woman turned to face me as my eyes widened in horror. It was Priestess Alisya, the mummified mother of

Cezar who had just been shipped to the states. A hiss escaped her lips as she placed her bony hands around my throat and choked me.

I woke up from my dream. I was still sitting in the filth from the flash-flood at the foot of the mountain; however, there was a boa constrictor squeezing the breath out of me around my neck. Lucky for me, I had a knife strapped to my right thigh. I stabbed and sliced at the snake. It soon gave up the battle as it slithered away."

Carl's heart pounded in his chest, imagining what this poor man had been through.

"I managed to hobble into town." Dr. Banner continued, his breathing heavy. "I had money wired to me as well as being granted to travel without my passport. I procured a ride to the airport with my trunk in tow. And so here I am."

"I've got to hand it to you, that was some story! Maybe you can write a book about your adventures some day," Carl conceded.

Dr. Banner never got to write that book or take credit for finding an exquisite mummy. During his flight, he experienced a heart attack and died. Priestess Alisya got her final revenge.

~ ~ ~

"Hi, my name is Timmy O'Malley. I 'spose for an eight-year-old, I have some pretty tall tales to tell." He paused to lick some ice-cream which was melting down his cone and onto the sidewalk. "My gramps was an archaeologist. He went all over the world digging up neat stuff. Sometimes he brought a discovery home with him." He paused again to give his new dog a taste of ice-cream. Timmy looked up and then shook his head as if to say *you're never going to believe thi*s.

One overcast autumn day, Timmy was home alone. While he played with his favorite action figures in his bunk bed, he heard a noise in the attic. An investigation was warranted. He switched on the light, at the base of the stairs, and walked up. Although the light was dim, he knew right where to go, beside the only window. Sure enough, there was a plump mouse with half of its body in a mouse trap. He would take care of that. He reached for an empty soda bottle and beat the mouse in the head until he was satisfied that it was dead.

"Ew gross!" he exclaimed as he tossed the bottle haphazardly.

He heard the crashing of glass when the bottle struck an old family photo that was framed. He ran to inspect the damage.

"Oh, crap! I'm gonna get it for sure when mom and dad see this!"

Timmy scrambled to find old coats and blankets that he could hide the broken picture. In doing so, he discovered an old trunk that looked older than him. He turned his attention to opening the trunk. Once the lid was open, he removed stacks of journals and maps. In the bottom of the trunk, Timmy discovered the mummy of a child that was wrapped in a hand woven blanket. A burial stone with intricate drawings was lying beside it.

"Woah, cool!"

Inside of the blanket was a scroll. It looked like perhaps his grandfather had taken notes on this old parchment from carvings at his archaeological digs. One note in particular began by explaining that the little Peruvian boy's name was Cezar. He was the son of an Incan priestess. Cezar became fatally sick and died. His mother cast a spell over his corpse and gathered some objects to resurrect him. It was also noted that her people became extinct for reasons unknown.

Another of his notes was entitled, How to Raise the Dead. There was a list of things needed:

> Black candles
> Incense
> Blood
> Singing bowl
> Bark
> String
> Water

"Directions: light your candles and incense. Wet the bark with water. Place the bark on the string like a necklace and then on the corpse. Smear the blood on the head and the feet of the corpse. Finally, chant repeatedly into the singing bowl these words, '*los muertos cobran vida.*'"

That was all that was written. Did his grandpa plan to resurrect this little mummy? Did he die before he could perform it? He sat there surrounded by the contents of the trunk thinking it over. Then he decided he would finish what his grandpa had set out to do.

Timmy lifted the mummy, still wrapped in the blanket, and set it outside of the trunk. Next, he cleared a space to place the black candles and incense. His parents warned him about playing with matches, but he kept some in his back pocket anyway. He found them useful for burning the ugly beetles he found in the garage. He lit the candles while smoke curled nearby from the incense. Timmy found a big piece of bark that was already strung on a piece of string in a plastic bag. Since he had no water, he spit on the bark and proceeded to tie it around the skeleton's neck. Blood was on the list. He walked over to the dead mouse. Using a scrap piece of paper, he scraped some blood off of the floor and smeared it on the head and feet of the mummy. As Timmy held the singing bowl in front of his face, he began to say the chant over and over.

There was a sudden rush of wind. The attic went dark. A strange rattling noise echoed in the darkness, almost like a wind chime made with…bones. Timmy struck another match to find himself face to face with Cezar. Timmy jumped backward in fright, but he was soon overcome with fascination.

"Hi, I'm Timmy. I don't know if you can understand me, but I want to be your friend," he said as he placed his hand on his own chest. Cezar mimicked the gesture. "That's great! I bet you're hungry after being in that trunk all this time." After realizing that Cezar had no functioning stomach he murmured, "You probably don't have anywhere for your food to go. That's okay. You can still come with me to the Dairy Queen."

Timmy helped Cezar down the attic stairs and into his bedroom where he dressed him in a T-shirt, Marvel Comics superhero pants, and a baseball hat. Off they went down the sidewalk in the direction of the Dairy Queen. All of the sudden, a pack of neighborhood dogs surrounded little Cezar, pouncing on him all at once. The clothing flew in all directions as Timmy helplessly stood by watching. Each dog took an arm or a leg from Cezar which left him wiggling in the street with one arm attached to his head. Just then a huge Culligan water truck ran over what was left of Cezar and killed one of the dogs. Timmy was devastated. No one would believe this story. He proceeded to walk to the Dairy Queen, to drown his sorrows with a large chocolate dipped ice-cream cone.

I wonder if that spell would work on a dead dog? He sighed.

AFTERWORD

By Glenda Reynolds
Author of

Curse of the Incan Mummies

The story Curse of the Incan Mummies was built onto another short story titled Dying to be Your Friend written for a 2013 "October Skeletons" monthly writing challenge at Linkedin. I wanted to keep the theme of a Peruvian boy brought back to life. I then had to change it from skeleton boy to mummy.

The initial tale needed a back story: enter Dr. Ollie Banner and the curse he unleashed. I enjoyed researching ancient mummies of Peru while writing this.

It is a privilege to continue to participate with my fellow writers each month at Writers 750 at Goodreads. You can learn more about me and my published works at http://glenda-reynolds.weebly.com.

Two Men and a Van
By Glenda Reynolds

"You have a visitor," announced the prison guard to the raven-haired young man in the cell. Shane was alert, as his eyes riveted from the floor to the man in the green suit, behind the sliding cell door. The man stepped inside the cell, nodded to the guard, and then came to stand next to Shane, as the guard closed the cell door with a loud clink.

"The name is Nathan Fitzpatrick," the man said and extended his hand in greeting. Shane gave him a firm handshake. Nathan glanced at the tattoos that graced Shane's arms: on the right inner forearm were the words "BAD TO" and on his left forearm were the words "THE BONE".

"I hear that you've been arrested on several counts of aggravated assault," Nathan said, glancing back up at Shane, "and destruction of property. I'm here to represent you as Counsel."

"What are you really? A fairy? I could smell you down the hall before I even laid eyes on you."

"I am in fact a leprechaun, but a lawyer by trade," he said with a twinkle of his blue eyes. "There *is* fairy blood in my veins. I know that is very appealing to supernatural creatures such as you." Shane's eyes widened. "Oh, it wasn't hard putting two and two together: large scratch marks at the scene; a man who claims that a large hairy beast with teeth and claws attacked him; and a very big pile of poop, marking your territory, no doubt. So tell me, from the beginning, what happened."

Shane relaxed and leaned against the wall on his jail cot.

"It all happened about a week ago. I was sitting in Pappy's Bacon Bar & Grill, throwing down some brews, when I heard the ladies talking at the next table. The pretty one, Jade, said that she needed her furniture moved to Birmingham in a jiffy. Well, I had just gotten my new moving van for my new business venture, Two Guys and a Van. I hadn't yet gotten a tax number from the state or even proper insurance for the business. But when I heard that Jade needed a mover, I thought that it was quick money in my pocket. I immediately offered my services. I made her a sweet deal for $1,000.00 even. Billy and I would help her box her items, load them, and ship them to Birmingham."

"So what happened next?"

"I came to find out that she is a collector of antiques. I wasn't prepared to box and ship fragile items like these, things that can't be replaced. I also didn't have proper moving pads to do this job. Remember, I still had things I needed to do since I just started this business."

"In other words, you jumped the gun on this one."

"That's exactly right! So here we got 'er all packed and moved. She wanted it all to go to a rented storage unit for the time. When it all was unloaded off the truck, she pointed out some vases that had been broken. There were a couple of pieces of furniture with damage too. Jade refused to pay me what we had agreed on. Her two ugly friends Tamika and LaErica were there, making matters worse. They all got up in my face. That's when I turned."

"Turned into what?"

"I'm a were-tiger. I sprout whiskers, fur, claws, teeth, the whole nine yards. Before I turned all the way into the were-tiger, I poured gasoline on her furniture and set it on fire." Nathan's jaw dropped as he continued to listen. "Who was the person that I assaulted?"

"That would be your partner, Billy Bowden; although, he has refused to press charges against you. I'm sure that charge will be dropped."

"I don't understand. I usually have full control over my ability to change. It was as if something or someone had power over me that evening."

"Bear with me for a minute. Do you mind taking off your shoes?"

Shane got a very puzzled look on his face. He slipped his work shoes off and handed them to Nathan.

"Just as I thought," he said as he pointed to the insole, "someone has hexed you with satanic inverted pentagrams inside of your shoes."

Nathan ripped out both of the insoles and burned them on the floor. Then he replaced the insoles with some of his own that had the Celtic Trinity knot emblem on them. Shane put his shoes back on.

"I'm sure that we can have this case dropped for you. No jury in the world will believe that a were-tiger destroyed some furniture, let alone drove the moving van. There is another matter that I'd like to discuss with you." Nathan pulled out a box of gold coins from his briefcase.

"What's this for?"

"These gold coins serve two purposes. One is to pay for your bail. And the other involves a personal matter.

You've been courting Laura Fitzpatrick, right?"

"Yes, what about her?"

"I'm her father. It's good to finally meet you. I would like the two of you to have a little nest egg to start your lives together. You know how that fairy blood is so appealing to you supernaturals."

With a twinkle in his own eyes, Shane replied, "That's exactly right!"

"Well, I'm off to represent other "supes" and to argue other cases. Keep your nose clean. Don't remove those shoe insoles that I gave you. They will help control the beast inside. If you do, you'll have to answer to me. I'll be giving this box back to you once your bail is posted."

The two men shook hands again as Shane said, "Thanks for everything."

After Shane was out of jail, he got his moving van out of impoundment in order to drive home. There was a note under the windshield wiper.

I know where you live.
Jade

There was a large paw print beside her name.

AFTERWORD

By Glenda Reynolds
Author of

Two Men and a Van

I have been influenced by southern author Charlaine Harris when it came to this short story. I enjoyed reading about the "supes" or supernatural creatures of the Sookie Stackhouse series.

I did this short story for the March Writers 750 challenge that had to include a Leprechaun. It is also partly based on a true story told to me by a co-worker as far as the fate of the furniture that was being moved.

It is a privilege to continue to participate with my fellow writers each month at Writers 750 at Goodreads. You can learn more about me and my published works at http://glenda-reynolds.weebly.com.

~ ~ ~

The Gifts
By Sojourner McConnell

Long ago, the people of Hill Valley lived in small mining communities. Every day, around the clock, men enclosed themselves in an iron cage and dropped deep into the mine. The trip took several dark, tension filled minutes. The blackness surrounded them like a damp blanket. In the cage were dozens of other men that came from the same place in life.

It was a place of sadness and poverty, a place of want. Dreams? Sure they had them at one time. But the coal and the dust kind of pulled it out, leaving in its place a husk of the former man.

This is the telling of the events of one such man, Darrell McGee. This husk of a man was solely responsible for the feeding, clothing and nurturing of a family of three children. He had his two girls, Mattie and Connie and his one son, Elliot.

Darrell didn't like to think about the babies that had come and gone before. He didn't want to remember the little ones that had not had a chance. Those babies had broken the spirit of his beautiful wife, May Belle, and left in its place a sad, weak woman. The last baby had taken her away. He did not place all the blame on them, well not so much that he felt guilt about. He simply wanted his May Belle back.

It had taken over a year for Darrell to mention her name without tearing up. The tears would well up in his eyes and he would rush to his room, so that no one could see. He felt that he had lost everything. The three children were a constant reminder of that loss. He wanted to feel more for them, but he just couldn't. Not yet, anyway.

Each morning, Darrell came home from the mine and would get the children off to school. Sometimes he would sleep most of the day; most times he just rested and napped. Darrell was a man that desperately needed to recharge.

Just over a year after May Belle's funeral, Darrell was rocking in her favorite chair by the fireplace when it happened. He can't tell you to this day what he was thinking about. But suddenly the wind kicked up in such a fashion that it lifted the curtains completely up and over the rod holding it in place. It wrapped itself so tightly that the room was vividly bright with the midday sunshine. He shook his head in wonder as he saw his beloved May Belle standing right in front of him. Her face as rosy and healthy as she had been on the day they married.

May Belle was a fine figure of a woman. Ample bosom and small waist with hair that dropped almost to that small of her back, and her skin as pale as butter. Then he saw her bright green eyes and the smile that said, "We have some work to do here."

Darrell gulped and blinked owlishly at his bride. Was he seeing things? Darrell wanted this to be real, but he was now worried that he had just lost his mind. He felt that there was no way his May Belle could be back. Yet, this is what he had prayed, begged and bargained with God for. All he ever wanted was his May Belle back.

Darrell began to search through his memory for what exactly he had offered God, if he could just have her back for one day. His soul, his children, money, what had he promised?

Darrell was still sitting in the rocking chair. His hair, oily and tangled in his lack of care, reached his shoulders now. He pushed his locks back. A part of him felt happy, but a bigger part felt afraid. Very afraid. He felt doomed.

May Belle was standing calmly in front of him, hands clasped in front of her, waiting. She looked the picture of patience, just as she always had. She still held that sweet smile on her lips, and she did not seem at all concerned that he had yet to speak to her.

When Darrell stood, he towered over the small thin woman. His six-foot frame was heavy with muscle, obtained from using a pick and shovel deep in the ground.

"Is that you, May Belle?" He was still gulping in nervousness, making it hard to be understood. "Are you real? How did you come back? Oh lord, I have missed you so much." Once he opened his mouth, it all came out in a flood, all the questions that had been whirling around in his head.

May Belle had not spoken a word and Darrell wasn't sure what to say next. He wanted her to know how much he had missed her and how much she meant to him, even today. The year she had been dead had not lessened his love for her.

He reached out to touch her and she stepped back one step. She shook her head at him. There was no dismissing that message. She was not to be touched. Darrell dropped his hands and forced himself to stop moving closer.

"Alright, May Belle. What do you want? Why are

you here?" Darrell's voice was clear and firm now, he felt comfortable in his own sanity for a moment, knowing this was real. His beloved May Belle was back.

May Belle walked around the small living room filled with the dusty furniture that she had pieced together from helpful family and friends. It might not be much to look at now, but it had been theirs.

"You are not taking care of what was ours, Darrell."

May Belle finally spoke and her voice carried over to him like the wind. Not the happy loving voice of his memory. This voice was unnatural, chilling him to the bone.

"The house? I am not much for dusting and sweeping. You know that."

He held his hands up in a frustrated motion. Confused as to why she would be so concerned about the dust and cobwebs of the little company house. Heck, they never even owned it. The Mining Company did. They were allowed to live there as part of the package deal that the new union had worked out. He did not care about this little house. Why would she worry about a little dust and a few mice?

Her whispery voice gained a harsh tone, like the rumble of distant thunder.

"Darrell! Think. Why would I come back about a ramshackle house? There is a greater problem. I am here for your salvation. Not your holy soul, but the salvation of the man you have become."

Wearily, May Belle shook her head. Her annoyance at Darrell was a tangible thing in the room. Darrell looked stair, his mouth hanging open. He had no idea what she meant. What was she referring to when she said 'his salvation?'

"Stop speaking to me in riddles," Darrel pleaded with the almost translucent woman. "Tell me what you want from me. I pleaded for you to return to me and pick up where we left off. I wanted a wife to hold and love, not a preaching woman."

The ghostly rolling eyes should have been a warning to Darrell, but he did not take notice. He was only concerned with how his prayers had been answered, yet it was going all wrong.

"Speak what you mean, Woman!" Darrell was shaking now. He felt out of control and he felt like he was being reprimanded. He had done his best. He had returned to work the day after the funeral. He was bringing in groceries and clothing when it was needed. What more did she expect from him?

There was a crackle in the air, the walls began to throb, and the wind howled. Darrell looked around the room in terror.

What the heck is happening?

The bright sunlight that had announced May Belle's arrival was all but gone. Instead, the room was filled with a heavy vapor that threatened to surround the couple. The darkness was increasing by the moment.

Darrell could feel the chill all the way to his bones. Wrapping his arms around himself, he tried to warm his tired body. His eyes were wide and his skin had grown pale.

"Gifts!" She shrieked, the voice sounding nothing like her own. The former patience erased from May Belle's rosy face. Her face was now gray and sullen. The anger was practically shooting from her eyes like torches in the mine.

"You squandered my gifts! I left you three precious gifts and you squandered and neglected them." With each word the roiling in the air increased.

Darrell cringed at her tone and her words.

"These three gifts were all I ever had of value in my short life, Darrell, and you have not appreciated them. You have one chance to start over. Will you accept this opportunity? Or will you squander this as well?"

Her look of disgust and disappointment tore through Darrell. Was she from the devil? His May Belle never spoke to him like this. Her voice had always held love and respect for him. She had always spoke gently and lovingly.

"Who are you? Where is my May Belle?" He did not believe her. He was fighting for his sanity. He did not want to believe this shrieking spirit was his darling May Belle.

The now wispy form danced in front of him, swaying back and forth before she responded in an exasperated voice.

"Where is the loving father of my children? Where is that gentle man that helped me with all of the heartbreak? The lover that filled this little house with love and care, where is he?

Darrell was shocked. Had he so changed? Had he lost himself when he lost May Belle? He refused to accept that he was not the same man he had been. He knew that he did not spend as much time with the children as he should. He then admitted that he spent no time with them at all. How had he not noticed that?

Was this wraith truly here to help him see the error of his ways, the mistreatment of his children? He loved Mattie, Connie, and Elliot. They had always been there with him, helping him in the barn with his little projects.

They happily greeted him in the mornings when they would wake and find him seated at the table having a bite to eat before sleeping. He vividly remembered spending time with the three little children before May Belle left. Sadly, now, in looking back over the past year, he had no memory of doing anything with them.

Shocked with this revelation, Darrell simply dropped into the rocker. Pushing with his feet, he rocked as fast as his brain worked to unravel this mystery. How had he lost himself? How could he make it up to the three of them?

His fingers drummed on the arm of the chair as he organized his thoughts.

The howling wind slowed and only gusted on occasion. He just now noticed that the windows were all closed on this chilly fall day. He wasn't able to process all the terrifying events that were taking place, but he could feel the truth taking shape in his heart. The love he felt for Mattie, Connie, and Elliot built into a warm fire in his soul.

"Oh, May Belle, what have I done? I missed you so much. I grieved and still grieve for you. How could this have happened? I am so sorry." His heart was heavy, yet strangely his mind was alive. For the first time in a year, he was thinking clearly. Darrell was thinking about the past, the present, and the future, with hope.

He felt fear, that was true. He also felt a great change come over him. How had he not realized that his precious children were a gift to him from his May Belle?

He would never again blame them for her death or resent their surviving. He only wanted to make up to them for the lack of love of the past twelve months.

He looked up at May Belle and saw that she was even more vapor than a person now. She had been slowly fading as he searched his heart. He was going to lose her once again. Only this time, he felt at peace. The terror was fading, as well.

"Thank you May Belle, Thank you for the gifts. I will treasure them. I swear that to you." Darrell continued to thank her until she had completely faded from sight. All he could feel upon her disappearance was a sweet, homey spirit about the house.

Standing up, he hurried to the kitchen and pulled out May Belle's old feather duster from the cabinet under the sink. He began at that moment to whisk away a year's worth of dust and cobwebs from each room. He felt no need for sleep. He only wanted to have a clean home when his children, his gifts, returned from school.

When Mattie, Connie, and Elliot entered the sparkling clean house, they immediately noticed the delicious smell emanating from the kitchen. All three looked around in awe at the changes. It looked and smelled like home, back when their mama was alive. They didn't know what to think. They went through the house looking at the neat rooms until they found their father in the spotless kitchen.

"Dad?" the three children said at once. They could not form any other thoughts at that time.

They wanted to make sure it was their broken and sad father in front of them. He no longer looked broken and sad. He looked radiant.

What miracles he had accomplished in just the few hours since May Belle left him. He did not share his haunted afternoon with the children, he simply assured them that they were never again going to be forgotten and neglected by him.

Darrell knelt in front of the children pulling them into his warm embrace. He spoke openly and honestly to them for the first time in a long while.

"I hope you can forgive me. I love you all so much. I will be the father you deserve, from this day forward. A father your Mother would be proud of."

For the next twenty seven years, he did just that. May Belle would never have reason to return and chastise him again.

AFTERWORD

By Sojourner McConnell
Author of

The Gifts

This story comes from being raised around the small mining communities in Alabama. As a child I would see the small pointed roofs and wonder about why they all looked the same.

My Grandfather would explain about the mining community and the company owned home. The miner's and their families had a hard life. This story reflects one family and their struggle.

I have had one book published and am preparing for publication of my second novel. "The Shepherds of Donaldson Park", due out in the summer of 2016.

I hope you enjoyed *The Gifts* by Sojourner McConnell. If you would like to know more about my works in progress as well as my current and past book reviews, please visit The Page Turner at https://vickgoodwin.wordpress.com.

Tell Your Truth
By Elaine Faber

He sat in the corner of the University library, as was his daily custom. He chose the spot where the sun, shining through the stained glass window, would warm his back as he sat, eyes half-closed, never moving, apparently unnoticed by all who entered the library.

He stirred around noon, when two men, young Gordon Jacobs and Tom Gibson, came into the library and moved behind the volumes on world geography.

He knew them well. He often watched the men when they came to read, to whisper together, sit with friends, or research a class paper. From their conversations, he determined they were dormitory roommates and attended classes at the university.

As usual, they paid him no heed as he sat quietly, listening to their banter, observing them without intruding on their conversation. It's safe to say they never even noticed him watching from the corner.

Today, the two men argued. Which of them should take a particular girl to the New Year's Eve Dance? Did she favor the tall man or the short? Did one have a right to claim her over the other? Who met her first and was that a deciding factor?

The argument escalated until, in a rage, the tall man struck his rival. The victim fell, striking his head on the corner of a library table. He lay motionless as blood pooled beneath his head and oozed into the flowered carpet. Without looking left or right, his friend rushed away, leaving his friend to live or die alone.

It happened so fast, the witness was powerless to stop it. He was horrified by what he had seen, but there was nothing he could do now. He sat frozen in the corner, waiting to see if the man was alive or dead, waiting for someone more capable to come to his aid. He slipped quietly away when help arrived and young Gibson was declared dead.

Greatly troubled by what he had witnessed that day, he said to his wife, "I saw what happened. Shouldn't I tell someone what I saw?"

His wife begged him to keep his silence. "If you come forward, it will make trouble for all of us. You know how they feel about us. We don't speak their language. With his father's social standing, no one will believe you anyway, even if you could make them understand. Please, just stay out of it. My dear, I fear for your life if you tell what you saw."

The next day, the newspapers decried the murder and, within days, the son of a poor family was arrested. He was seen in the library shortly before the murder. He was known to have a grudge against the victim. He must be the guilty one. In a violent response to the murder, the townsfolk screamed for vengeance. Protesters marched on the jail house with firebrands and guns, crying for a quick trial and speedy conviction. The young man was sure to be convicted and hanged for the crime.

The community was shocked to learn, the next day, that the young man was released and Gordon Jacobs was arrested. Wasn't Jacobs the victim's best friend? How could it be that he was now accused of murder?

A reporter from The Daily Clarion rushed to the police department, seeking a story for the newspaper. Why the release of one man and the arrest of another?

"How could we hold an innocent man?" the detective on duty explained. "We have irrefutable testimony against the guilty man. Apparently, there was an eye witness to the murder. Come and see for yourself. The evidence only came to light this morning at the scene of the crime. You'll have a story to end all stories, and though it will amaze your readers, many may not believe it."

The reporter asked, "What evidence could you possibly have that would convince you of Jacob's guilt even before he's been brought to trial?"

"It's too fantastic. You wouldn't believe me if I told you. You have to see it with your own eyes. Here, in the library. See for yourself. Over there, in the corner."

"Where? I don't see anything. What am I supposed to see?"

"Look up!"

In the corner, with the afternoon sun glinting through the stained glass window, the witness sat where he had spent so many mornings, and where he had sat, unnoticed, on the morning of the murder.

He sat in the center of a giant spider web, which was stretched from one corner of the room to the other. Ingeniously woven into the center of the web were the words, "I saw the murder. Killer was Gordon Jacobs."

AFTERWORD

By Elaine Faber
Author of

Tell Your Truth

Tell Your Truth - I wrote this story so long ago, I can't remember just what inspired me. Many of my stories are either about animals or written 'by' the critter involved. What must they think? How do the events affect them? Hearing the story from the critter's point of view vastly changes the telling of a tale.

In *Tell your Truth*, a critter witnesses an event of immense proportions. How he tells his truth to alter an injustice becomes the climax of this unusual story.

If you like this concept, you will enjoy *Black Cat's Legacy, Black Cat and the Lethal Lawyer,* and *Black Cat and the Accidental Angel*, where, Thumper, the black cat with his ancestors' memories, helps solve mysteries. My latest humorous mystery is *Mrs. Odboddy - Hometown Patriot*.

Read more about my stories at
www.mindcandymysteries.com

Monster in the Box
By J. Rene Young

Abigail Smith and her husband Blake had recently purchased a quaint, four-bedroom home, in a quiet Midwestern suburb. It was a dreamy little cream-colored house with a two-car garage and a fenced backyard. There were just enough trees to give adequate shade without sacrificing space for outdoor activities. Today, they were taking personal time off from their jobs, as an insurance salesperson and local contractor, to finish unpacking and settling into their new home.

Blake worked tirelessly to haul in cardboard boxes from the garage in the sweltering late-summer heat. Abigail found herself in their son's room, admiring her handiwork after she had finished putting together Jeremy's new play tent in the corner beside his bed. Their six-year-old was attending his first day of school and his parents wanted him to come home to a bedroom fit for a first-grader. Abigail smiled at the layout. The new bookshelves beneath the window would be perfect with a nice padded seat and a few pillows thrown in. She then scooted the empty dresser beside the door over an inch or two so it would be closer to the bed in the corner. Standing back again, she basked in the warm and fuzzy thought of her son playing happily here.

"Here are some more boxes with books, I think," Blake said, grunting as he dropped the load beside the door. He looked around the room. "Looks great, Abby. But where are Jeremy's toys going to go?"

Abigail frowned at the empty space she had

inadvertently created beside the closet door. "Hmmm, you're right. We need to get him a toy box next chance we get."

Blake returned to the garage while Abigail started unpacking. Before long, Jeremy's bookshelves were full and his tent had been populated by stuffed lions, tigers, and bears.

"Oh, my!" she said, giggling at herself when she realized the tent was overflowing. She pulled a few animals out and arranged them on Jeremy's bed, then got to work on his collection of toy trucks.

"Abby!" Blake's voice echoed from the garage. "Come look at what I found!"

In the garage, Blake was stooping over an old wooden chest, the hinged lid lifted as he examined the inside. The chest was rugged, crafted from reclaimed planks of varying colors and grains, and was about three feet long, two feet tall, and two feet deep. Abigail raised her eyebrow at the light cloud of dust that flew up when Blake let the lid fall closed.

"Did the old owners leave this here?" she asked.

"I guess so." Blake clapped his hands to clean off the debris. "There's nothing inside but cobwebs, so they probably aren't missing it. It'd make a great toy box for Jeremy!"

"It's nice," Abigail said, not entirely sold on the idea. "Maybe, if we clean it out, sand it down, give it a nice stain —"

Blake waved a hand, mainly to help the dust cloud dissipate. "Nah," he said with a cough. "It's nice as it is! It'll give Jeremy's room a more rustic feel."

With a sigh, Abigail conceded. "All right, but clean it out before you bring it in the house. I don't want any bugs coming in with it."

Shortly thereafter, Jeremy's new toy box was snug beside the closet door, across from his bed, filled to bursting with the majority of his stuffed toys and cars. Abigail and Blake had finished pulling in boxes from the garage. When the afternoon came, a little boy hopped off the bus in front of their house and ran inside with his backpack jostling against his tiny shoulders.

"Jeremy!" Blake cried, yanking his giggling son up into a ferocious hug. "How was school today?"

"Good!" Little Jeremy's big brown eyes beamed. "My teacher is really nice and I made some new friends today!"

"That's great, sweetie!" Abigail said, giving her boy a kiss on his cheek. "Well, Mommy and Daddy did a lot of work in your room today. You should go see your surprise!"

Jeremy gasped and struggled against his dad's arms. He ran down the hall, making happy noises as he padded toward his room. Abigail and Blake followed behind, smiling at each other. All summer Jeremy had begged them for a tent for the backyard, but until now they hadn't had the space. Jeremy was sure to shout when he saw the one Abigail had set up in his room.

But there was no squeal of excitement. Not so much as a peep. Frowning, the Smiths came to the door and were met with a strange sight.

Toys had been hurled all over the floor, under the bed, and on the bookshelves and dresser. Some items Abigail had put up on the walls, like picture frames and the letters in her son's name, were skewed or had fallen completely down. Jeremy's bedside lamp was lying on his pillow, the shade cocked to the side from the fall. Jeremy stood in the middle of the room, his brown eyes wide, staring at the toy box. The lid was up and its contents were gone, clearly strewn across the room. Jeremy still wore his backpack on his shoulders.

Abigail's mouth dropped open. "What happened?" she asked quietly. The little boy did not move, his eyes trained on the box beside his closet.

"Jeremy!" Blake raised his voice. Jeremy jumped and looked at them, his expression panicked. "Why are the toys all over the floor? How did you do that so fast?"

Jeremy's eyes got wider and he glanced toward the box. "But—"

"Did you throw a fit or something?" Abigail asked, her heart falling at the disappointing scene. "I thought you'd like your new set-up."

"No, Mommy, I didn't throw a fit," Jeremy answered, his voice soft and trembling as he began to stare at the box again. "They were already like that."

Blake stepped forward and grabbed Jeremy's backpack from his shoulders and dropped it beside his bed. The boy's eyes never left the toy box. "Jeremy, don't lie to us. You know better than that."

Abigail sighed and shook her head. "Honey, go talk with him. I'll clean this up."

Blake steered Jeremy out of his room and down the hall while Abigail kneeled to reach the toys that were under the bed. The father and son entered the living room and sat together on the couch. Jeremy was breathing quickly, his little chest heaving up and down.

"Jeremy, why did you throw your toys everywhere? We worked really hard on your room, and that hurts our feelings."

"But Daddy, I didn't do it. There's a monster in that box. The monster did it."

Blake sighed. "Jeremy, there are no such things as monsters, and even if there were, they don't hide in toy boxes."

Abigail listened to her boys talking in the living room while she cleaned, then decided to examine the toy box. The inside was completely empty. No spiders or bugs or anything even remotely monster-like. She let out the breath she had been holding, dumped the toys back into the box, and closed the lid again.

~ ~ ~

The first morning after, Abigail walked into Jeremy's room and it looked like a disaster had struck. Toys were everywhere again, but books and clothes were also tossed around the room. Jeremy was sitting up on his bed, curled around one of his tigers with his back against the corner of his headboard and the wall. His lamp was on his pillow, and to Abigail's horror a trickle of blood could be seen trailing down Jeremy's temple. After that, she removed Jeremy's lamp and decided to leave his bedroom door ajar so that they could hear him more easily from down the hall.

A few days went by and Jeremy began acting strangely. The first night after they had set up Jeremy's room, he refused to brush his teeth. Next, he refused to put on his blue shark pajamas, followed by his refusing to get into bed. All the while, the little boy kept saying, "There's a monster in my toy box!"

This became a daily occurrence and soon Jeremy refused to let Abigail return his toys to the box. Instead, he set each of them up on the floor around the edge of his bed, saying they'd help keep the monster from getting to him. All of this worried Abigail sick, but Blake kept saying it was just nerves from school.

"He's just trying to get used to his new school and new house," Blake would say. "It's a stage all kids go through when they move. He'll grow out of it soon enough."

But every night, when Abigail tucked Jeremy into bed, the terrified little boy would whimper the same phrase: "Mommy, please, there's a monster in my toy box."

Abigail didn't know what to do. She felt like her son was being terrorized by something, but she had a hard time accepting anything that had to do with a monsters in toy boxes. Finally, exasperated, she sat down on Jeremy's bed.

"Look, sweetie," she said, holding his tiny hand in hers. "Your dad is right. There is no such thing as monsters. You need to go to sleep."

Jeremy's skin was cold from fear. "But mommy, there is! There really is a monster in my toy box!"

Abigail was beginning to lose her patience. She lurched off the bed and stomped over to the closed toy box.

She lifted the lid and, as she had expected, the box was empty. No toys, no bugs, no monsters.

"See, Jeremy?" she said, her annoyance seeping into her voice. "There is nothing in this box. I love you, okay? But it's time to stop this nonsense and go to sleep."

"You just can't see it, Mommy, but it's there! There's a monster in my—"

"Stop! Stop." Abigail startled herself with how loud she had gotten. She breathed, walking back to Jeremy's bed. "Okay. I'll talk to Daddy, and we'll see if there's something else we can do, okay?"

"O-okay," Jeremy whispered as his mother leaned down to kiss his forehead. She turned off the light in his room, but left the door to the hallway open. Her footsteps were muffled by her slippers as she walked down the hall.

Jeremy lay in bed, his brown eyes wide open, soaking in the light from the hall. His tiny heart was pounding in his chest and he could hear his own rapid, ragged breathing in his ears. His mother's footsteps faded away, and silence filled the room. That unnerving buzz that comes with silence became more prominent as time passed. Jeremy could not close his eyes.

There was a rustling from somewhere in the room. A cold wave of anxiety swept over Jeremy's small body. He could feel the prickling of the hairs on his neck and arms. He held his breath.

THUNK.

Jeremy sat up and stared at the toy box. Its lid was still closed tight. Jeremy was rigid, unable to move, unable to breathe. Terrified.

Silence.

THUNK.

~ ~ ~

Abigail flopped onto the couch into Blake's arms, exhausted.

"Maybe we should just get rid of that box," she said, snuggling against her husband's chest as he watched the television. "Sell it, give it away, something. Jeremy obviously doesn't like it."

"I still think he's overreacting, Abby," Blake said, flipping through the television channels at random. "Maybe he feels like we aren't giving him enough attention and this is his way of getting us to spend more time with him. You know, tomorrow, we should all get out of the house and go to that amusement park we saw in the next town over. I think Jeremy would enjoy that."

"Yeah. You're probably right."

They sat in the quiet of muted commercials for a moment. Then, a series of short, high-pitched shrieks came from Jeremy's room. With her heart racing, Abigail sprang to her feet. Blake followed behind as he muttered how this was getting out of hand.

The screaming stopped before Abigail reached the door. She whirled into Jeremy's bedroom as she threw the door wide open. The light from the hallway spread across the room, washing over the bed, where she could see her son. He sat on a pile of sheets with his eyes unblinking and a finger outstretched toward the toy box.

"Oh, Jeremy," Abigail said, letting out a whoosh of air. "Why did you scream like that? You scared me half to death!"

"Mommy, there's a monster in my toy box," Jeremy replied, staring back at her with a blank expression.

As Blake reached the door, Abigail rolled her eyes and stomped over to the box once again. She reached for the lid.

"Jeremy, I told you, there is no monster in your—"

She froze, stopping in mid-sentence. She had lifted the lid and set it back against the wall. Inside the box was a little boy, dressed in blue shark pajamas. He lay curled into a little ball around a stuffed tiger with his eyes squeezed shut. He opened his eyes, big and brown, and looked up at Abigail.

His voice trembled.

"Mommy? Is the monster gone?"

AFTERWORD

By J. Rene Young
Author of

Monster in the Box

As a little girl with a heightened imagination, I often found myself thinking about all the "What if"'s that come with playing alone in a huge, unfamiliar house. The fear of the unknown and the noises in the dark, along with the fear that what you see is not as it seems, have played a large part in writing my first completed scary short story.

The "monster" is based on a changeling or doppelganger, which typically tries to replace the person it copies by making him or her "disappear" somehow (usually by eating the victim or changing it into something else). I like to think that the boy Abby found in the box at the end is the real Jeremy, but I left it open to the reader's interpretation.

I have been writing for as long as I can remember, but until now I have not had the opportunity to be published. I have reached a point in my life where I can finally focus solely on my word-smithing, and I have a number of projects in the works that I plan to have ready for publishing soon.

Closer
By Joe Stanley

I)

I had once been a dashing, handsome man. My words could make men and women smile and laugh with joy. I knew a second childhood in those gatherings of us, the young lions. Of wine and song and, best of all, of women, I knew much. Our band of friends was strong and seemed a bond stronger than even that of blood. I preferred them in their best moods but had nursed them in their tantrums. Those of us who withstood the merry vigil were rewarded to watch the rising of the sun. There is magic in those moments that might outshine all the secrets of the stars.

What blessed angel brought her to me, or why, I know not. From that instant I laid eyes upon her, there could be no other. My gaze must have betrayed that yearning so painful. I feel I must have, for eons, already known its frantic distress. Without so much a word between us, our eyes made vows that moment. As I grew to know her, it was more like remembering. I whispered once that our meeting was but reuniting and we shared our tears for the sweetness of its truth.

My own good name and the prestige of my family earned me the blessing of her father. But even as I made special plans to ask her for her hand the world crumbled. She was gone. She lived no more. I would not accept it. They say I was mad with grief. I cannot recall. I do remember friends coming round, trying to draw me back into the world. But in those sparkling lights and tinkling melodies my heart would seek her out. I'd glance around, so certain, for I felt her there still. My eyes would find her not and I'd remember, she was gone. Thankfully, there were no more parties when I proved a burden to the band. I was no longer who I had been.

In the endless dragging of days, I hungered for death to take me to her. Would it not condemn my soul to Hell, I'd take my own life. Surely, she had gone to paradise, so suffer on I must. I filled my days with books. To her memory, I would read what words of love I'd find. From the library window I watched a year pass. I exhausted the library and would gather books as I found them scattered elsewhere through the ancient house. I learned the storied history of our venerable line from journals, memoirs, and diaries. I learned of the estate and its nebulous customs that were otherwise beneath me. I floated through the halls being little more than the whisper of a breeze.

In the long unused chapel, above the family crypt, the great book, and notes on its lore of death, waited to offend me. The book had said that living know that they will die, but the dead know nothing. I beg to disagree. I should prefer to think that she, somehow, can feel my yearning just as I still feel her in my heart. The soft light, filtered into colors by the stained glass, lit the gathering attended by grief, despair, and hopeless fury.

"What know you, oh resplendent Lord, but thy own hateful perfection? Dare you stand in my shoes, knowing only what I do? I had presumed that you watch over us, oh Creator, believing that we reflect the myriad within you. Perhaps I have, in error, disregarded the possibility that we are but the tiny and imperfect things that can dwell within thee not? Perhaps this world is Hell made perfect by appearing to merely be the earth? Just tell me that I am damned, if it is so. Just tell me it is alright to end this torment. And answer me you will not, so may have I surmised and spoiled thy secret?"

When at last my tears subsided, I turned from that hateful place and the repellent falsehood of its joyous, prismatic light. I stumbled back, through the dim and silent halls, to my chamber. The comfort there is spoiled by the vacancy on the bed beside me. I whispered into that void until sleep dimmed the world away. I longed to hear her voice, to know its melody. To the edge of consciousness, I lingered, passing through it to the faint tones of a harpsichord. Dare I dream I heard that whisper, "I... still... feel..."

II)

What pleasant dreams carried me through fields of eternal green, among the flowers countless and sweet, to the vineyards and orchards. Even the grumbling of the gray sky could not diminish our time. How we pressed together beneath those great limbs and emerald leaves, seeking shelter from the rain. Oh love, I have found thee at last only to wake unto this wretched life again. But there is more I must confess, as I search that happy memory. How sadly I must ask, have you been gone so long that I cannot recall your lovely face?

Such a wretched thing I am to fail you so. I vow, my

love, there is none but thee. Though your beauty is unequaled, it was in your heart that I found my hope reflected. Perhaps the face I wear now, so marked by time and tears, might be unrecognizable to you as well. But my heart, dear love, is everlasting in its yearning to know you and only you and for all of time. Let the centuries grind me to dust and my heart will still burn for you.

I stood beside the harpsichord. I did not know that you could play. I recall your love of music, should I be so surprised that you have learned? I sat where you must have sat the night before. I swear that I could feel you there. The silent air compelled me to touch the keys that knew your fingers and to imagine that I have thereby touched your hand.

If I feel you close, does that mean where you are is close? If I see you, will you show me the way? We are star-crossed for now, but the stars in their course follow a cycle. They shall become right again. Then, I will know you in more than dreams, in ways that death cannot change.

I walked the grounds. Each step upon the lawn, beneath the sun, felt wrong. It is because you are not with me. Without you, the trees become grotesque sculptures, vulgar in the writhing wildness of chaos pure. The beautiful home, without you, is but an effigy, crumbling beneath the weight of ages. The flaky dust of its foundations seeps into the soil and from that primeval muck raises its voice in a wordless tribute to the blasphemy of time itself.

I feel you walking in the halls. I race along the floors to find you but, time and again, I find nothing. It wounds me to know you are so close. Better that you might walk with me, that I may tell you of its history. Yet, I feel that you could tell me more than I may ever know. Somehow, you seem as much a part of this place as the stones it is comprised of. There are, I sense, reflections of you hidden in its features. Centuries have prepared it for you, as I have waited eternally.

Tell me love, what more must I understand? Does this fog, that has arisen, cloak thy perfection from mine eyes? Would that I could join you in that ephemeral, swirling dance. That our footsteps scatter the fallen leaves, that the trees would sway in time and with the grace we shared. May we dance until the sky itself becomes exhausted, for, in all its haunting vistas, there are no two lights as bright as yours and mine.

I ask again, what more must I understand? What secret keeps you from me?

III)

Once, long ago, there was a girl of incredible beauty. She was all that a lady can be. She knew the eyes of desire upon her but quietly declined the baser passion. For she awaited love. The choice of many suitors was hers, but she knew the man she sought above the rest. So much like my beloved, the hand of death bore her away too soon. For the loss of this youthful beauty, all wept. With her passing the world seemed a little colder, a little darker.

To remember her always, they called upon the monks to preserve her flesh. They, not by the grace of God, but by the means of alchemy obliged. By formula obscure, they concocted that which was to be called the blood of saints. They infused her with its immortality and stepped away. Days and weeks and years rolled by and her features remained as they were in life.

Time passed and her name was forgotten, but her beauty remained. When no one could recall where she came from or why, the monks claimed her as a forgotten saint. For all her radiance, they took her to a place of gloom and darkness. There she rested among the bones and leathery husks. Still, she was desired.

Those unholy men, who crept among the dead, ogled her with leering, hungry eyes. They committed their blasphemies in the candle-lit chamber of onyx. How dare they be so vile! How dare they desecrate her eternal rest! How many must have succumbed to her subtle temptation? Did they ever hear her whisper in that darkness? How many died by her daring request?

"Touch me..."

She had never known the warmth of a lover's hand. She must have died aware that she would never know. Her sleeping eyes, I wonder, do they still dream of its promise? Does her heart long still for the love it has never known? Does she desire to feel its light in her tomb of eternal darkness?

Still she rests in that underworld, in those catacombs beneath the family crypt. The ruins of the monastery may still be traced there upon the hill. I have gazed myself through her etched, crystal coffin and upon her beautiful face unspoiled from all those centuries.

The saints' blood is the method my line is still

embalmed with, though a modern man would cite the effective ingredient as arsenic rather than magic. It preserves the flesh indefinitely, but leaves it fatal to touch. It is but a parlor trick to the true magic of her beauty. I see now why it matters not that I cannot recall my beloved's face. In the hearts of men there is and can only be one, no matter which face she wears.

She is the embodiment of desire. All of nature is wrong to leave her to this fate. Farewell, my love, I shall see you soon. When darkness has fallen, when the moon has risen, I shall listen then for thee.

IV)

You are quiet as the moonbeams falling to the floor, yet I feel each graceful step that brings you closer.

In the soft voice of the breeze, I hear your whisper.

You are so cold...

I will share my warmth, my life with thee.

How I have longed to feel your cold arms around me, to taste your lips if but only once.

I shall want no more...

now that...

you are mine...

again.

AFTERWORD

By Joe Stanley
Author of

Closer

Where do these stories come from? That's a tricky question. I can understand why the ancients believed in muses, it certainly feels that way. The urge to write comes out of nowhere and soon disappears back there. I can only hope I've got it all down. Then, I wait for it to return.

Really, though, I've always been a daydreamer. With authors such as Poe and Lovecraft among my favorites, it's no surprise that I love a weird and creepy tale. These stories take place in a world I call *The Abyss*. It's a world much like ours on the surface, but one that holds key differences, as you will see.

Out of the countless expeditions I've made into that other world, occasionally, I come up with one or two I'd like to share.

Please feel free to visit me at
http://www.jonathanharker.co.uk/index.html

The Ghoul
By Joe Stanley

Smythe and Jaymes were the lowest of the low. They were ruffians and thieves and, some said, much, much worse. Between the two there were enough brains to stay ahead of justice.

But that is where the brains ran out. Throughout their partnership, an intense rivalry developed. Nowhere else was their competition as fierce as in romantic affairs. They kept count of their conquests, spending the fortunes they stole to outdo each other. But Jaymes fell behind.

Jaymes had found something special.

For this, Smythe taunted him relentlessly. More than once they nearly came to blows. While Smythe would visit brothels, Jaymes would seek his sweetheart. Though Smythe believed that his partner would come around, Jaymes only fell deeper.

And much to Smythe's dismay, Jaymes seemed to be reforming. He even spoke of settling down! How long, then, would it be until remorse set in and confessions were made? If confessions were made, how long until he implicated his old partner?

This wouldn't do. In the interest of self-preservation, Smythe had to put an end to it. First he tried to seduce Jaymes' beloved.

"In all fairness," thought Smythe, "Jaymes is but a poor specimen, what woman would want him?" Yet, that wench spurned his own advances and threatened to reveal them to Jaymes. So Smythe turned to the alternative.

One night on the docks, as they passed a bottle of rum between them, Smythe began.

"Brother, I've been unkind."

Jaymes stared and asked, "How so?"

"I've begrudged you, out of ignorance, out of jealousy."

Jaymes began to reply, but was waved off by Smythe.

"You have something I have never known, the love of a good woman. I don't think I'll ever have that, and I was wrong to ridicule it."

Silence.

"I think, my friend... Yes, I believe that you should retire. Settle down and make a life with the lovely girl you've found. You're strong and young and I think you can find work."

Jaymes was shocked, but smiling.

Then Smythe continued, "Too bad the pay is so..."

Jaymes nodded with a growing frown.

"I don't know how I'll get along without you..." and after a drink, "I've been thinking of reforming myself!"

"Good!" said Jaymes, "My brother, I'm glad you said that."

"I wish I had just a piece of the fortune I've wasted. It would make things so much easier..."

And, right on cue, Jaymes went on, "As do I."

"Too bad we can't pull off one more job... Might make settling down easier, but, no, I don't want to draw you back into it."

"Who says we can't?"

"Think of the ring you could give her, eh?"

"Let's do it!"

"Are you sure? I don't want to..."

"Damn it all!" Jaymes cried, "For my brother, one more is not too much to ask!"

Smythe laughed and said, "I've got just the thing, the biggest, and easiest we've ever done."

"I'm in."

"Hold on, now. We've..." and he leaned in close to whisper, "we've broken a lot of rules before, but this one is the biggest. For this last job, there will be no rules. If you can't swear to go in with me, I'd prefer to call it off, now." He sat back enjoying Jaymes' silence.

For a few long moments, Jaymes thought quietly. He knew that Smythe must have something terrible in mind, for Smythe never worried over breaking rules. But he had said it would be big and it would be safe. He finally broke the quiet, "For my brother, anything."

"Good man," replied Smythe, his twinkling eyes turned away.

~ ~ ~

The sun had hardly set as the two sped through the forest. They were twin shadows, stealing forth, slipping through the trees without a sound. They climbed a hill and crouched behind its top, peering over.

It was the Count's ancestral home. All the windows were dark. Since he died before the Revolution, this place was forgotten in that bloody uprising. Besides, his heirs had already looted its treasures.

They slipped down the hill and to it, gazing through the dusty windows to the vacant rooms inside. They went around it and left it behind. Ahead a grove of lush trees spilled from the hill beyond. Within the grove, shining in the moonlight, the marble entry way of the tomb loomed tall.

Jaymes put his iron into the frame. "God forgive us," he whispered and he strained until he broke the seal. The two pushed the heavy door in, heedless of the noise. A hallway led deeper into the hillside.

Along the length of the hall, the sculpted busts of the Count's line glared with scorn in their lantern light. It was as if they had foreseen this moment and had visited it on the sculptor. Such faces pronounce a wordless condemnation on those who behold them.

The hall ended in circular chamber. Columns rose to the ceiling. The murals, though faded, showed the glory of the extinct line. Hunting scenes, great battles, all but memories meaning nothing now. Between the columns were statues of angels, while both peaceful and stern they put the busts to shame.

"There, see," Smythe pointed to a large iron ring fastened to the floor, "Just like the other one old Willy told us about. A great stone stopper!"

For some time they worked to set up the block and tackle. And only by great effort could the two of them lift it from its recess. It swung back on hidden hinges and they fixed the rope to hold it in place.

"It won't do for it to come down," teased Smythe. They gazed down the stairs that might have run all the way down to Hades itself.

At the bottom, a corridor ran off to either side. "I'll have the right, you the left," said Smythe, "Take only the best you find, else it will be too much to carry."

So they parted to the grisly task. Along the walls in niches, the caskets of the dead awaited plunder. They snatched necklaces, yanked earrings out or fished them from the dust, and snapped brittle fingers to strip the rings from them.

Smythe, all the while, kept an eye on Jaymes, waiting for the moment when he slipped out of sight around a corner. At this, Smythe stole back the way he came and back up the stairs. Moving behind the great stone seal, he drew his knife and sawed slowly and carefully at the thick rope. As it began to snap he called down the stairs.

"Jaymes," he cried, "Oh Jaymes... Come quickly!"

"What? Where are you?" came the faint response.

"Up here!" he called again, "Best hurry!"

Jaymes appeared on the stairs while Smythe smirked down at him. He raised the knife. They stared at each other, now that both knew the score. Then the rope snapped and the great stone fell back into place.

The treachery of Smythe was far from over. In the early hours before the dawn, he stood over Jaymes' sweetheart and clamped his hand over her mouth. He savored the tears in her eyes, sparkling like diamonds, as he told her with a whisper, "Jaymes is dead. You will be too if you make a sound!" When he was finished, she was dead all the same.

The rumors of the savage murder made their rounds.

A woman dead, her lover missing... the rest took care of itself. Smythe stayed on only a few days more, just enough to avoid suspicion.

He left that place behind with a pouch of gems that kept him well cared for...

...for a time.

~ ~ ~

But what a time!

He traveled to many great cities. He drank the sweetest wines, and took them from the lovliest of ladies. Oh, the countless ladies! They were a feast to sate the beastliest desires. He wore the finest clothes, and he found that they suited him completely. He slept in the softest beds. He had minstrels and poets and parties the equal of which he had never known.

By shrewdness, his wealth long outlasted any he had ever held...

...but only for a time.

As it ran out, he found himself slipping back into the filth of the gutter. His friends, who loved to drink his wine, had none to spare for him. The ladies, who loved him so tenderly, couldn't even be bothered for a smile.

"Come back," they told him, "When you're rich again."

Their laughter came in a chorus as he was escorted to the gate and cast into the muddy street, fouling what remained of his finery.

"I will!" he spat, "Damn you to Hell! I will be rich

again!"

But no one heard him from the street except the passers-by. How their stony faces condemned him without a word. Slinking off to some wretched place, he managed somehow to beg himself a room.

In that lonely darkness, he thought of days long gone. His regret troubled him.

"If only I'd taken more..." he thought aloud. He licked his lips, "...but there is more!"

In the darkness, he smiled and drifted off to sleep.

His dreams might have been troubling to some, but he reveled in the horror show. He saw Jaymes, at the top of the stairs, straining and clawing at the stone. He saw him rushing through the maze of corridors, searching for another exit. He was frantic to find one before the lantern went out. But it went out and he was lost in darkness.

All the while, Smythe laughed at his partner, the fool he had once called brother. Then, the dream took him again to a place where tears and blood, pleasure and pain were an experience like no other.

He woke feeling better than he had in ages.

The trip was long, and he savored the anticipation of seeing that place again, of plundering the wealth that awaited.

He stole through the dark forest, beneath the moon. He slipped through the trees like a shadow. From the top of the hill, he peered down upon the Count's ancestral home. He gazed through its dusty windows to the emptiness inside.

Around it he went and found the grove. In the grove, the tomb loomed tall. The door, its seal still broken, he pushed open, heedless of the noise.

Within, the busts still condemned him, the angels still stood witness.

From his pack he removed ropes and a winch. With a match, he lit his lantern.

"Well Jaymes," he spoke into the emptiness of the tomb, "I've finally come back."

~ ~ ~

He cranked the winch and the stone rose much easier than it had with block and tackle. He locked it in place and checked it again. It wouldn't do for it to come down. As he walked around to the stairs, he almost expected to find him there. But nothing...

The stairs lead him down, and he stood where Jaymes had stood. He stared back up to where he had stood before. It seemed so long ago. When he turned and descended, a sight awaited his lamplight. The shell of his partner, his brother, slumped against the wall. Now it was but so much lifeless leather wrapped around bones.

He stood for a moment, half expecting it to come to life. Beside it, a pile of skulls stared up from the floor, and above them a message had been left. There, on the soft gray wall, was scrawled in dark letters...

"Smythe," it read, and an arrow pointed to the left.

"Poor man," said Smythe, "Oh, my poor brother, you brought it on yourself."

But as he turned, he noticed the floor was strewn with shattered bones. "Lost your mind, no doubt..." He crept carefully along until he reached the corner. He could remember Jaymes disappearing around it. Another step brought another pile of skulls and another message into view.

"I ate the dead," it confessed, and an arrow pointed to the right.

"God," shuddered Smythe, but he pushed on, with countless bones scattered by his steps. He chuckled, "If that will do you've had enough to last. But water, that would be your problem!" The next pile of skulls sat below the message... a question...

"Why did you kill me, brother?" it asked, and an arrow pointed to the right.

"To save myself, damn you!" he thundered into the dark. Every coffin seemed to have been spilled. He gave up his attempt to step lightly and crushed the bones beneath his feet. His fury was growing still when the next pile of skulls came into view, but its question stopped him cold.

"Why did you kill her?" it demanded, and an arrow pointed to the right.

"No," Smythe shook his head, "No, you can't know that! A lucky guess, a delusion, a visit from her ghost, what does it matter?" His rage flared back and he kicked the skulls down the hall. They clattered against the walls and rattled together in the darkness. His anger drove him on to the final pile of skulls.

"Treasure" it promised, and an arrow pointed to the left.

Here the bones were so deep that he stumbled. They tangled around his feet and he fell. By some luck, the lantern didn't go out. As he pushed himself up one of the bones caught his eye. He saw the marks left on it, scratches made by teeth.

He felt sick... and sorry.

But to his ears a sound made itself known. It was a familiar sound but it took him a moment to realize what it was and what it meant. "NO!" he screamed and scrambled up and on. He could have followed it with no light at all, but he had to see it to believe that it was real.

There ahead, a steady dripping left the floor wet. But his concerns were forgotten at once. Scattered and twinkling like countless stars on the slimy floor, was the accumulated wealth of the catacombs. He howled and cheered and stuffed his pouches with everything he found. And chuckling, he turned and traced his way back.

"Jaymes, you crazy fool!" he laughed, as he looked down at his brother, "I'm sorry it had to be this way. I'll thank you very much for collecting this for me. Indeed, I'll thank you when we meet again in Hell."

"One last thing," he said, and stopped to scratch his name off the wall below the stairs. When his knife had done its work and he could no longer read it, he smiled, but the voice that came from above him stripped it from his face.

It was more of a growl, or like swamp gas bubbling up from the muck.

"Smythe..." it cried, "Oh Smythe... Come quickly!"

"Who's there? Jaymes?" came his faint response.

"Up here!" it called again, "Best hurry!"

He scrambled up the stairs pleading, "Jaymes! No! Please! I..." but at the top of the stairs, there was no one. He stopped, dumbstruck. Then the stone fell, sealing him in. After some minutes of screaming and futile struggle to lift the stone, he turned and walked down the steps. There, on the wall, a new message waited.

"Eat," it offered, and an arrow pointed down to the corpse of Jaymes.

AFTERWORD

By Joe Stanley
Author of

The Ghoul

The Ghoul was an idea that came to me, one dark night, and insisted that I follow it. I simply could not refuse. It is a tale of jealousy, betrayal, and revenge from beyond. I've been a fan of ghostly tales for as long as I can remember.

It's been my great pleasure to offer these two to you. I truly hope you have enjoyed reading my short stories as much as I have enjoyed writing them. But for now, a knock upon my door tells me another story has come calling. I hope we meet again...

Please feel free to visit me at http://www.jonathanharker.co.uk/index.html

Anna, Child of Fire and Light
By Lena M. Pate

An infant lay swaddled in a ragged blanket within the dilapidated walls of a once proud and prosperous edifice. Now the building stood in ruins, rock mixed with choking vines and gnarled trees.

A lioness, on the hunt, heard the babe's mew. Her proud head lifted to sniff the surrounding area. The pitiful sound came from over by a rock formation. Thinking it might be an orphan kit, she was both surprised and confused to find a human child. Pacing back and forth, tail swishing with irate ticks, the lioness nudged the human cub with her nose. The crying stopped. A hand reached out from beneath the scraps of linen and buried itself within the warm, soft mane. No fear from this cub, just curiosity.

The regal dame knew the child needed nourishment, of which she couldn't provide, so she gently lifted the swaddling between her mighty jaws, traveling deep into the forest.

They traveled throughout the night, the babe sleeping soundly. She knew where to take the child. The cub would be safe with her own kind. The old woman would take in this orphan, just as she had other sick or injured creatures. Most returned to the wild, fully mended.

Prudence woke early this day. A premonition infused her with energy and foresight. She was to receive a child this day. How or why she did not know. She boiled linens and towels in castile soap, milked the goats, prepared the nutrients to make a usable formula, and boiled the bottles and nipples used to nurse small creatures. While hanging up the wash to dry, she was startled to see the large cat approaching with something clutched in her jaws. The rumble from her mighty chest was a warning. Prudence stood still.

The lioness only encroached just past the tree line before placing the bundle on the ground. Having delivered her package, she disappeared into the dense cover. Prudence waited, but curiosity got the better of her and she approached the package with care. The bundle moved, boding well if there were any injuries. She heard the mewing and she wondered what type of cat was wrapped in the cloth. Leaning over, she gingerly pulled aside one fold and then jumped back in shock. Before her lay a girl child, whose eyes favored the blue of the sky and hair as crimson as the setting sun.

Prudence assumed that some dim-witted fools thought that the child was a changeling and that the fairies had stolen their child. Much more likely, the mother had slept with more than just her husband. Best way to justify the odd child was to claim the fairies took their baby. Humans could be so cruel.

"Well my radiant angel, whatever shall I call you?" On the way to the cottage the name came to her.

"I shall name you Anna, after my deceased sister. She was always full of joy and mischief." As she entered her kitchen she noticed the date on her calendar was October 31st. "Well, I'm not sure if you are a trick or a treat. Although your name will be Anna, I shall nickname you Pumpkin, after the season and your bright mop of hair."

During her warm bath, Prudence noticed a birthmark on her shoulder of a half-moon surrounded by freckles that resembled stars.

"This is the reason the suspicion was laid upon your head then. They believed you were spawned by the devil. We must always keep this covered. To show this would mean certain death."

She wrapped the babe in a sun warmed blanket and sat in the rocking chair by the fireplace to feed Pumpkin the prepared goat's milk.

"Slow down you little piglet!"

But Anna would have none of that. She drank the entire bottle and then made bubbles with her mouth, laughing at her cunningness. Prudence sat a small wooden crate next to her bed. She made the child a mattress by gathering goose down that she kept stored for new pillows.

Anna, what shall I do with you? She pondered while she knit. She was an old woman who lived far from the village. Prudence was known about these parts as a witch. Being a changeling was one thing; being the child of a witch was a burning offense. Prudence tended to stay away from others unless they came to buy a curse, a spell, or to end a pregnancy. They came bearing gifts for bits of herbs and oils. Her final decision was to raise her.

Pumpkin grew to be a fine looking woman. Prudence taught her everything she knew, for she was getting old and Anna would soon need to take her place. Every once in a while, they would spot a lioness at the edge of the tree line and were certain it was the cat that had left Anna. She would come by to check on her. Nature was kinder than mankind.

It was on a brisk winter's day when Prudence called Anna to her cot.

"Pumpkin, you have been such a blessing to me these many years. I am proud of the woman you have become. You are so willowy and beautiful, like a summer rose or the burnt autumn leaves. I fear I must leave you now. All that is mine is now yours. The villagers have become used to you being here as my apprentice, so they will keep coming to you for their needs. When I am gone, will you place my body beneath the old oak tree by the river? That is why we dug that deep trench before the winter set in. I will rest peacefully there."

Anna clutched the woman's hand as she passed to the other side. Now there would be no more lessons, or chats, or games by the fire during long lonely winter nights. There would be no one ever again to call her Pumpkin. That evening, with a full moon to light her way, she wrapped Prudence in her burial shroud and carried her to her resting place. Anna laid rocks atop to keep the animals away. Her tears froze on her cheeks. She felt nothing but numbness.

As she turned toward the cottage, she noticed the old lioness approaching. They looked at one another for a moment, then the lion went to the graveside and lay across the rocks, guarding her old friend. Anna smiled. Who better to watch out for Prudence than the aged cat? They will more than likely share the same resting spot one day.

A few weeks went by and Anna received several villagers. They all asked after Prudence, and even though they knew Anna, they were unsure how much to trust her with their secrets. Anna had a way about her though that soon won them over. But soon the snows were deep and she knew that no one would come again until spring. It would be a long cold winter alone. There was not even an animal to keep her occupied. Prudence never believed in keeping animals as pets. Once they were well, they were sent off to live in the wild where they belonged.

One blistery evening, as Anna returned from gathering wood for the stove, she noticed movement close to the back of the cottage. Thick woods bordering the hut helped to buffet the winter winds. Setting down her load, she carefully made her way towards the back with her lantern and large walking stick. The snow was thicker on this side of the house where drifts gathered. As she approached, her light reflected off of a handsome pelt of a young gray wolf. He lay on his side, his breath coming in puffs, and his chest laboring for each breath. She knelt close to him. There she stayed, quietly observing her new patient to gain his trust. Slowly, she reached out her hand to allow him to sniff, then stopped when she heard the snarl and noticed him bare his teeth. He didn't move otherwise nor attempt to strike, so she held still with hand outstretched, giving him the ability to determine her friend and not foe. After several long moments, she moved a bit closer. He watched but did not move.

"You must be very injured to allow me such liberties. I will not hurt you. I am but a healer wishing to help. I must examine the extent of your wounds then see if I can move you indoors."

Eventually, the wolf dropped his head back onto his paws and allowed her to gently stroke and touch. For being outdoors in this cold, he was exceptionally warm and weak. When Anna tried to roll him, he snapped in her direction but did not bite. It was then that she noticed the congealed blood pooled beneath his body. One wound appeared to be on his belly, towards the right side, and another went through his hip. If she didn't tend to him soon he would surely die.

Anna retrieved a wooden slab with ropes tied to one end and straps about the board to secure him. With great care and caution, she slid the board beneath the wolf. She placed over him wool blankets and empty feed sacks before strapping him to the plank.

"You have given up haven't you? You aren't even attempting to bite me now."

She carefully made her way around the cottage and up to the front door. Prudence had made a ramp beside the steps for this very purpose many years ago. A sheet of ice lay beneath the snow aiding her in the task of getting him in out of the cold.

She settled the wolf near the fireplace, exposing his injured side. A bullet had gone all the way through his belly but Anna's exam found no organs damaged. It was the hip that worried her. She would have to operate and remove the bullet, clean the wound, and apply ointment before it festered. She managed to persuade him to drink warm milk laced with valerian powder and hops.

As he fell into a deep sleep, Anna cleaned the wound, sterilized her knife, needle, and thread as well as a pair of tweezers. She shaved the hair and cut open the hip. The bullet had imbedded itself into the bone. By the time she removed it and stitched him up, she was so exhausted her hands and arms shook. She had to secure him to the board again, so he wouldn't move and break open any of the stitches or bandages. Deciding it was better to sleep in the den, so she could hear him stir, she gathered her bedding and slept on a cot near the kitchen.

As the sun rose through the window, she awoke to a commotion. It took a moment to acknowledge what she was witnessing. Her wolf was changing into a man, as naked as the day he was born. She loosened the straps and covered his nudity with her afghan. The transformation was soon complete, but he was still too sedated from the medicine and his loss of blood. She realized that what she had was a werewolf in her home, not a natural animal.

Preparing for him to awaken, she boiled chicken to make stock and soup to appease his hunger. The broth and some herbal tea would help him the most at first.

She sat mending clothes and sheets as she waited for him to wake. Near noon, his body stirred and his eyes opened to show beautiful gray orbs staring back at her. He quickly took in his surroundings but didn't speak.

"You do have a tongue. I remember seeing one when I doctored you," she said with a smile, setting down her mending. "Could you use something to drink?"

A gravelly "please" followed by a distinctive growl alerted her that he despised being at her mercy.

Snatching the food from her hands, he took refuge in a corner, his blanket barely covering his necessities. At first, he burnt his throat gulping the broth, then began to sip from the bowl and cup instead.

"If you break open my handy work, I shall be quite

displeased. Move closer to the fire. I will see if I have anything that will cover you until you feel better.

She rummaged through an old trunk, locating a man's shirt and pants in a deep midnight blue. She also located a pair of heavy knit socks, which most likely had once belonged to a hunter Prudence doctored.

While he dressed, she went back in the kitchen to make him another bowl of broth with a bit a chicken this time. She knew he wouldn't like it much, but she added medication to help him go back to sleep. He needed rest more than anything at this time.

"What is your name?" she asked.

"Where am I?" was his response to which she explained about villages within walking distance from here.

Soon he slept and Anna spent the day redressing his bandages and checking his stiches. Much different than when he was a wolf. She had never been this close to a man before. His physique was finely honed, with strong muscles in his back and legs. Probably due to his curse, she thought.

As night fell, she deemed it safe to put up a screen and bathe.

She stood in a sizeable tub and was rinsing her hair and body. The tresses were long and wavy wet but curled tightly when it was dry. As she stepped from behind the screen, the sight of him awake startled her. The long sheet she used to dry with drooped off one shoulder exposing her birthmark.

"So you are the missing changeling. The story says she was left to die in the ruins of Gladmere, but instead her body was spirited away. Everyone thought the fairies refused to make the exchange because she was marked with the sign of the stars and moon. But here you are, all grown. I imagine the witch found you and kept you well hidden. If anyone were to ever see your markings though, you do realize they would most likely burn you?"

"As you are aware of your fate, I too know mine. So, now that you know of me, what will you do?"

"Nothing, I owe you my life. You also know my secret. Yet you do not fear me. I say we make a good match, don't you, my sweet pumpkin?"

She gasped at the endearment.

"Your hair and freckles remind me of autumn and the pumpkins that grow ripe in our fields."

She nodded but made no hint as to why this surprised her. "I shall doctor you to health, but then you must be on your way. It is the way I was taught. We do not keep what does not belong to us. Their fates belong elsewhere in this world."

So the werewolf, whom she discovered was Alan, prince of the realm of Hollowshire, recovered and left before the next full moon.

Two years went by and he never returned.

Anna, however, now found herself locked in the stockades of Gladmere, to be burnt on the night of the next full moon.

She remained strong, refusing to cry or beg for mercy. These same people, that she had treated over the years, now accused her of heresy and devil worship. A couple had come to see her about a potion to rid the wife of a babe she carried. She was so near her time for birthing that

Anna refused. Angry and suspicious of her red hair and blue eyes, the husband reached up and tore away her dress, exposing the birth mark. They dragged her to town, to be tried and sentenced. She had no fear of death; it was a natural fate for all. What made her sad was that she would never see her werewolf again. Since his departure, she thought of him daily, hoping he would return. But no one could come to her rescue now.

The night came, the full moon lighting the way to the ruins of the castle. It seemed fitting for her to die where her life started. There would be no lioness to save her this time. The proud cat died, as Anna had predicted, lying on top of Prudence's grave.

The tormentors' torches blazed a trail through the darkness. They secured her arms to a pole with rope, laying twigs and dry timber at her feet. The magistrate and the cleric both read the charges. Stoic through all the lies, she closed her eyes, awaiting her fate.

Flames consumed the smaller, dried branches on the outer edge quickly and the heat rose as the townsfolk chanted, "Witch!"

Then she heard the screams.

Upon opening her eyes, she watched the people scatter across the countryside, leaving her to burn. She felt the rope bindings give way. Something dragged her from the flames by her collar. When she regained her footing, she turned to find a slightly singed gray wolf. He escorted her to a cave, where they spent the night.

As morning dawned, bright and golden, the man who had been wolf held her close. "You said you do not keep what does not belong to you, but my heart has belonged to you from the first. Ours fates are one, and we belong in this world together."

As he held her, she heard him whisper, "My lady pumpkin."

She smiled and snuggled into his embrace.

AFTERWORD

By Lena M. Pate
Author of

Anna, Child of Fire and Night

Anna, Child of Fire and Night is one of those stories that bits and pieces came to me in the middle of the night. I jumped up, wrote them down, and then filed them away for use at a later date. This story can be construed as being from the past or even from a village in our day and time.

Superstitions, lore, and fear of the unknown, yet fascination too and homeopathic medicine are as common now as they were eons ago. Each of us has a match, our soul mate or other half, regardless of our faults or differences. These are what make us unique and, through love, we can overcome.

I have read and written since I was able to pick up a pencil or a book. My imagination has served me well, taking me on adventures, allowing me to keep the child inside alive.

My blog, lenasstoryandpoetrycorner.blogspot.com, is filled with poems and short stories.

I have been included in eMagazines and anthologies such as *Whitechapel 13, To Capture a Nightingale, Violet Hopes The Luck of the Shamrocks, Of Past and Future, Blow True the Winds* and an eBook titled "Following the Scent". I am about to publish a fantasy, "They Called Her Alivia –The Quest for Twelve Amulets", that should be available by June 2016.

Forever Mine
By Lena M. Pate

A scream ripped the fabric of darkness surrounding the small figure sitting ram-rod straight in the middle of the bed. The covers had fallen, revealing a sweat soaked nightgown and a heaving chest of a terrified young woman. Her eyes lay deep within bruised sockets. Whimpers escaped her lips after the immediate terror ended.

She tried counting how many nights this had been happening, but her fear kept the numbers at bay. Tossing the restrictive sheet and quilt, she scrambled from bed and donned a heavy robe. Now beyond the initial fright, the soaked cotton nightie resembled a slap of cold water against her bare skin. She slid her feet into a pair of warm moccasins and shuffled like an aged woman.

When she flipped the switch on in the kitchen, fluorescent bulbs pierced her orbs, rocketing pain through her temples and the frontal lobe. With trembling hands, she pulled out a carton of milk, and sloshed it over the side of her large coffee mug. As she waited for it to warm, she removed cocoa, vanilla, and cinnamon from her spice rack. The sound of the beeper from the microwave startled her, causing her to drop the container of sugar. Stretching to reach her cup, she scalded her fingers on the porcelain handle. She retrieved Aloe vera and squeezed out the slimy gel to doctor her wound. She then proceeded to combine extra cocoa and brown sugar to the soothing warm drink. She extracted a pint of whiskey as poured herself a generous ration into her cup.

Struggling to drown out the panic she experienced after each episode, she snuggled into her favorite chair to sip her drink. The migraine came next. She iced down her head while sitting in the den and listened to soft, soothing music. No words; just notes that danced in the air.

I'm either crazy, dying of an aneurysm, or suffering from a massive brain tumor.

It was time to make an appointment with Dr. Maximilian, her doctor slash brother-in-law. Her older sister Rachel snatched him up while he was still in college. The man was handsome yet nerdy, introverted and studious. He lacked in social skills, but he had the heart of an angel for his bedside manner. Since they settled into the quaint town of Cottonwood, Catherine decided to go to him for all her issues that weren't feminine in nature. She imagined that seeing his wife's baby sister in "the altogether" would be a conflict of interest not to mention a bit awkward for both of them.

"Stacy, hello, this is Catherine." Catherine could hear the TV in the background and Stacy chomping on gum in her ear. "Hey, when are you coming in for your annual?"

"That's what I'm calling about. I need a bit of extra time with Max. I've been having trouble sleeping and starting each day with a migraine measuring seven on the Richter scale."

"Can you be here by 3:30 this afternoon? He had a cancellation, and that would make you the last appointment of the day. He can take all the time he needs that way."

They hung up, promising to have lunch soon when Catherine felt better. Rachel, Catherine, and Stacy had been inseparable growing up. Her older sister didn't mind her tagging along with them because of their strong bond. When they were kids, they hid in closets and under beds together, trying not to earn the wrath of their drunken father. They learned quickly to watch each other's backs. At least Rachel had married a good man.

Catherine took a long soak in a hot bath laced with rose water and glycerin. She must have fallen asleep. In her mind she heard him calling, taunting her to come to him.

"Kathy, my love, come join me. You know you want to. Stop resisting."

A sob escaped as she cringed from the demanding boom of his voice. Catherine could barely shake her head in answer; terror froze the words in her throat. She bashed the back of her head on the porcelain, coming close to sliding under water. Three thirty couldn't get here soon enough. Maybe she should pack an overnight bag just in case she was admitted; to a hospital, that is, and not a sanitarium.

"My goodness, Catherine, why didn't you come in sooner," Dr. Max asked without looking up from her file. "This disruptive sleep pattern and dreams are playing havoc with your system. Your BP is high, your ACTH and cortisol levels are extremely elevated, you have lost ten pounds since I saw you last, and you are physically and mentally worn out. You must get sleep. Your body will shut down without it."

"Honestly, Max, don't you think I would if I could? I've taken every over-the-counter medication, tried sensory therapy, and meditation. Do you think I'm crazy? Do I have a brain tumor or what?"

Patting her hand, barely able to look her in the eye, he told her it was too soon for a definitive diagnosis.

As they walked into the reception area, Catherine noticed Rachel flipping through magazines without stopping on a page. Looking up, she ran and gathered her into her arms. "Sis, what is wrong with you? You look about to keel over. Look at those circles under your eyes. Sit down. Sweetie. before you fall down."

She turned and ordered Max to fetch Catherine a cold glass of water. Appearing displeased, he bristled. Catherine noticed his hands bunched into fists in his pockets. "How strange," thought Catherine, "Max never loses his temper."

"Why do you order Max around like a paid servant. Don't you realize what a good man you have? He doesn't drink, smoke, stay out late, nor has he ever raised his voice at you, let alone his fists."

"He is so good it is getting boring. His head is always in books or scanning through dead patient records as if he could somehow bring them back to life. He says he is learning from past mistakes."

"You aren't cheating on him are you?"

Before Rachel could answer, he was back with a glass of ginger ale over ice. "This will help settle your stomach much better than water." Rachel appeared cross. Catherine was concerned for the two of them. Why, if she had someone as wonderful and smart as Max, she would never venture elsewhere.

Two days later, Max dropped in to check on her, with Rachel glued to his side. Rachel may not want him anymore, but she didn't want anyone else to take him from her. Rosa, their cook, had been kind enough to send potato soup and crusty bread. Catherine attempted to eat but chewing took more energy than she could muster. She pushed the chunks of potatoes around and broke off a piece of bread while Max stared holes through her.

"You are making me feel like a specimen on a slide, my dear Max."

Clearing his throat a bit, he looked at her and said, "My dear child, I'm only contemplating what we should do next. I believe you are in a vicious cycle. No sleep brings on headaches, which in turn, brings about the nightmares from the pain. I think the only way to get over this is for you to be put to sleep."

Catherine choked on a piece of bread she had soaked with broth. Rachel's eyes flashed daggers at her husband. "What a horrible thing to say to Catherine. Put her to sleep, really? Don't you ever think about what you are about to say before you say it? Now, before you blunder again, please explain what you mean by that remark."

"I meant exactly what I stated, dear. I'm going to place Catherine in ICU so she will be continuously monitored and put her into an induced coma. When she gets to the part in the dream where she usually awakens, she will instead face her fears, and wake up refreshed. She will have given her body a much needed rest. She will stop having the migraines and will have gotten past the issues surrounding this dream. I feel it is brought on by her horrific childhood."

"That was my horrific childhood also, dear husband. You don't see me carrying on so."

Catherine gasped and her sister had the decency to pat her hand and apologize. Max, convinced all his plans were going to be followed through, stood up and put on his wool coat and hat. Catherine hugged her sister goodbye. Catherine was very afraid but she didn't question the doctor. Max would never do anything to harm her.

The sky, that morning, arose cloudless and sunny with just a touch of autumn's chill. Catherine took a taxi to the hospital rather than driving. Straight away, she was wheeled to the fifth floor. The nurse's station sat in the center, and pods made of glass windows fanned out like flower petals from the receptacle. Catherine took note of the squeaky shoes rushing to and fro, beepers sounding off in various rooms and moans as well as screams coming from a few occupied cubicles. The smell of bedpans and disinfectant were enough to give one a case of the gags.

White walls blended with starched white sheets and a stiff, white cotton bedspread. The rest was taken up by monitors, oxygen, tubes, lines, and cords running from the wall and equipment. There was a bedpan chair made of recycled and disposable corrugated paper pulp right beside the meal tray. The only color relief in the room was the blue of the blood pressure cuff and the bed liners.

Panic encased Catherine, making it near impossible to move. She held onto the metal of the sliding door as if it were her life line. She felt certain that, if she crossed the threshold, she would never come back.

"It's alright, sis. I plan to stay right here with you until this ordeal is over. I insisted that Maximilian have the staff bring me a recliner to sit and sleep on for the next couple of days. You aren't alone."

Catherine advanced into the room, steadier knowing that Rachel would be there for her. By the time she changed clothes, a parade of doctors and nurses came and went, taking her vitals, poking and probing, looking into her eyes with bright lights as if to see what was happening in her cranium.

By afternoon, IV's flowed, monitors clicked off the beats of her erratic heart, and sensors connected to her scalp recorded her brain waves which were displayed on a screen. As the oxygen hissed, it reminded her a bit of her dream world, but she couldn't remember why. It seemed appropriate that today was Hallowe'en.

Max was having a heated discussion with someone in the hallway. After several words were exchanged, Max introduced her to the young anesthesiologist, who would be administering the propofol into her system.

"I want it on record that this is highly unorthodox to do this to a perfectly healthy woman with no brain trauma. I want no blame to fall on me if something should happen."

"I understand Harvey. I plan to keep her monitored and administer medications to keep her blood pressure up and flowing. If there is even a small chance of a problem, I will turn off the medication immediately and bring her out of the sleep."

"Max, you never said this was dangerous."

"Sweetheart, we use this drug every day to put people to sleep for procedures and surgeries. Why there was a patient once who was kept under for six months."

"Yes, but she had brain damage." The young man

leaned over to listen to Catherine's lungs and heart. Catherine smiled into eyes the color of milk chocolate, but there was only worry in return.

"Are you going to administer the medication, or do I need to call in someone else?"

"No, I'll do it. I don't want someone else flubbing this up." Harvey turned to Catherine and finally smiled. "This won't hurt a bit."

Catherine felt the cold drug enter her arm, smelled a faint odor of chemicals in her sinus, and then total, peaceful oblivion.

"See how peaceful she looks. The medication is being fed into her intravenous solution, and we can either give her more as needed or less."

Rachel resumed her vigil over her little sister. Why had she never noticed how frail she had become? Catherine was such a warrior growing up. Many a time, Catherine took the licks that were meant for Rachel.

"I have a tougher hide than you do," she would say, and then gingerly sit on pillows for days.

Night enveloped a moonless sky. Rachel stood staring out the window when she heard her sister moan.

"I'm here Catherine," she said as she took her hand and felt her forehead. *Sweat but no fever thank goodness.*

Deep within the darkness, Catherine could feel the monster chasing her. She heard his voice within her brain.

"What do you hope to accomplish, my little one? You can't hide from me. You carry me in your mind. I see, I feel, I taste everything you experience. We are one, you and I. Come on back, Kathy."

Catherine picked up speed as she crashed through the underbrush. Her clothes were torn, with dried blood matting her hair and trails leading to her ear. Her lungs burned and lights danced before her eyes. When was the last time she ate? Her fingertips were bloody from when she used her nails to dig her way out of the poorly constructed shed. Scrapes stung her back from the ragged boards she squeezed beneath to make her escape. He entered the privacy of her mind, taunting her.

"You are my property, given to me by God."

How was he able to get inside her mind? Would she ever get far enough away from him for the voice to stop?

"You know the answer to that, Kathy. Once bound, our chains can't be broken. I am with you always. Stop your running, Kathy."

"I'm not Kathy you fool. My name is Catherine, with a C. You are mistaking me for someone else." The wheezing in her chest and the stitch in her side wouldn't let her run any longer. She didn't even know if she was heading in the right direction.

"Tired yet, Kathy? Lie down on the ground and I will bring you back home. Sleep Kathy. I am waiting for you."

Catherine was nearly blinded by the erratic lights and zigzags dancing in front of her vision. It made her dizzy to try and focus for too long. Leaning over, she heaved. Sides aching, her stomach rolled and pitched, but all that came out was foul bile which burned her throat. She'd be damned if she would give up though.

Staggering forward, she stumbled over rocks and branches that lined the small path she had been following. She collapsed to the ground, scraping up her already bruised knees. As she regained her foothold, her feet began a descent down an embankment. She grabbed but found nothing but loose rock. She felt her body turn and now she was falling head first into the abyss. There was nothing before her but blackness.

"Here is where I wake up. Come on brain, wake up. Why isn't it working this time?" she spoke aloud, hoping to help awaken her body, but she continued to fall.

She could barely make out a floor. Squinting, she noticed squiggly lines bending and blending. Tails, then bodies appeared. *Oh lord, it is a pit of snakes.* She opened her mouth to scream but no sound came. She could see the pointed fangs, and the serpent's tongues, ready to strike.

She ducked her head and prepared to roll when her body slammed into the group. The bodies cushioned her fall. When she finally stopped rolling, snakes covered her. Hissing was so loud she could barely think. Hissing, like she heard once before in a different life. The fangs dug into her arms and legs. A few sank into her neck. Then there was blissful silence.

Morning came, and Catherine snuggled into her pillow. She felt too tired to wake up yet. Strange, her bed felt different. The sheets were silky smooth and bunched beneath her like small pillows.

"Might as well get up and take a long soak in the tub.

Oh, and a strong cup of coffee. Maybe I will even splurge and put cocoa in with some cream. She smiled and opened her eyes. Instead of sunlight pouring in through her blinds, there was nothing but pitch blackness. The air reminded her of freshly turned soil from her garden. As she began to sit up, her head hit something solid, causing her to fall back on the bedding. Reaching up, she felt a hard, rounded surface covered in the same silky cloth that covered her. The walls were the same on both sides. Where could she be? Then it dawned on her. She began screaming and scratching, her fingernails breaking and bleeding as she attempted to dig through the lid.

"You will never leave me again, Kathy. You are mine for eternity."

"Max, wake her up this instant. She surely can't survive this nightmare. Turn off the sedative and let her wake up."

The young man ran into the unit and started disconnecting all the lines. He administered medicine by slamming a needle into her heart. By then, the screaming had stopped. He rested his ear to her chest but heard no sound of air moving or a heart beating. Tears fell as he held her.

Rachel screamed and her husband gathered her into his arms. He let her cry as he rocked her against his chest, making soothing sounds of comfort.

The anesthesiologist looked up and overheard the doctor whisper, "You're mine now, Kathy; forever mine."

AFTERWORD

By Lena M. Pate
Author of

Forever Mine

About *Forever Mine* - I wanted to construct a recipe for terror that combined the moods and thought processes of both Edgar Allen Poe and Alfred Hitchcock with a sprinkling of Twilight Zone for spice. This Hallowe'en cauldron begged for a tale that layered suspicion, mystery and terrifying phobias. Death is easy. It is surviving man's insanity and ability to justifying their lunacy that personally scares the hell out of me.

I have read and written since I was able to pick up a pencil or a book. My imagination has served me well, taking me on adventures, allowing me to keep the child inside alive.

My blog, lenasstoryandpoetrycorner.blogspot.com, is filled with poems and short stories.

I have been included in eMagazines and anthologies such as *Whitechapel 13, To Capture a Nightingale, Violet Hopes The Luck of the Shamrocks, Of Past and Future, Blow True the Winds* and an eBook titled "Following the Scent". I am about to publish a fantasy, "They Called Her Alivia –The Quest for Twelve Amulets", that should be available by June 2016.

CHILLING TALES FOR ADULTS

Stories that may leave you
to wonder
whats under the bed
and in the closet.

Retreating Fog
By C. Baely

The storm outside was loud as it rained heavily. The sounds of the wind traveled all around the dark room and the windows sounded like they were cracking under the heavy thrust of the whistling air outside. Thunder broke above, in the night sky, and grew louder as the time passed slowly. Irene was in bed, feeling alone. There was not another sound in her room except her heavy breathing. The effort she made to simply rest, exhausted her. Something bothered her. A strange feeling that this night would not be like any other night. It was a nagging, anxious feeling, a deep consciousness that made her stare towards the draped window beside her bed. She was being summoned by the lightning strikes to rise and look deep into the storm. Irene pulled the covers higher under her chin. She disliked the feeling of forcefulness which pressured her unresting mind and yet for some strange reason she couldn't seem to be able to ignore it.

A voice, soft and inviting, sounded in her mind.

"Rise and come to me."

Someone called her. She could swear she heard it. Thoughts of impending madness made goose-bumps rise on the lower back of her neck. Cold chills ran down her sweating spine, while a soft tremble shook her body uncontrollably. Another attack of her illness; she was already drained from the bleeding. If anyone had seen her bathroom earlier, they would ask where was the body she had mutilated since blood covered everything. She spent hours cleaning the toilet seat, the floor, and the sink in order to sweep away all the blood she had lost again. Now she lay exhausted from her efforts.

Thinking she would soon fall asleep, she remained stubbornly unmoving under the warmth of her covers, wishing this night would go away, as many others had before this one. She stayed motionless in the dark, trying to calm the loud beating of her heart, when the voice that called her spoke louder in her mind, making her freeze in fear.

"Don't be so stubborn, Irene. Rise and come to me."

A nauseating feeling rose from the depths of her bowels, forcing her to twist uncomfortably beneath the covers as another spasmodic attack grew from within her stomach. She threw the blankets away from her and ran blindly towards the bathroom as she emptied her mouth from the sickening bile rising.

"It will be another long night," she thought in despair as she bent over the toilet seat.

Dragging her feet, she headed once more towards her bed. A crack of thunder broke the silence of the night while flashes of light ripped her room, making it flicker like a burning candle. She needed to breathe. Suddenly the air in her room wasn't enough. Irene walked towards the long draped doors leading to her small balcony. Her hands now shook with a chill like none other. It traveled up her shoulders to her neck and moved down her spine, making her grow colder.

She pulled the long drapes bringing her face near the icy glass. She breathed deeply near the window, creating a soft shadow of white fog from her breath on the cold glass.

She didn't like rain; she didn't like storms; she didn't like nights such as this one. It burdened her soul more than she could understand. It made her feel sad and lonely inside.

She looked ahead at the tall trees rising above her second story window apartment. They moved violently with the air slashing the soft leaves from one side to the other. For a moment, she felt that was her, as hopeless as the soft leaves of the tree being thrown from one side to the other aimlessly. With such force that it left her without a breath. Without anymore will to fight. With no more will to live.

All she had to do was open those doors, take several steps onto that watery ledge, and then move outside the protective bars. It would be so easy to let go. It would be easy to simply set herself free from this world and just take the plunge. A single step and everything would be over. No more unpleasant thoughts. No more torturous pain. No more feeling sick and drained from any will to live.

"It was all just a thought," she said to herself, and yet now she felt the cold air on her skin.

She felt the cold drops of rain whipping her face mercilessly. She felt her gown being blown by the winds as they seemed to be pushing her back on the rails she was now holding. Gazing down, it was a long drop from where she was standing. All it would take was one last step, just one little step - and let go.

She raised her eyes to the sky above and whispered in the winds, "take me with you, please."

Her hands rose up high into the dark night, and her body was free to fall. It wasn't even a leap to her death. It was just a fall of acceptance that covered her soul like a protective veil. She simply stepped away from clinging to life. The wind forcefully blew against her as if trying to stop her speeding drop. It was so cold, so very cold, like the last hug of death around her body.

"Soon," she thought, her mind at peace, "soon it will all be over." She closed her eyes and waited for the impact of the hard stone concrete beneath.

~ ~ ~

Irene took a sharp breath. Her head was hurting her terribly and she had a dry taste of bile in her mouth. Her back felt like it was being poked at in different places from burning needles dipped within her skin.

Strange. She tried to focus her eyes and realized there was no light around her. When did the storm end and become so quiet? She, tried to make out any shapes in the room. But nothing. It was pitch dark.

She exhaled slowly, trying to calm her rising heartbeat. She looked around her, unable to see anything or hear anything. When she placed her hands beneath her, it was as if she was sitting in an empty space of nothingness. She felt nothing but air. She breathed slowly as she tried to get a grip on herself and her horrifying thoughts of what had happened this strange night. For some reason, her mind had gone blank. All she could remember was standing before her bedroom window and then she woke up here.

Wherever here is.

A sound reached her alert ears and she turned her head sharply to her left, where the noise had come from.

However, she couldn't see anything except an abyss of black nothingness surrounding her. She had made an effort to focus on something like the door of her room, her small toiletry furniture placed at the bottom of her bed, or her balcony door, which allowed moon beams into the room on her right. There was nothing there to see, only the depths of deep darkness. Her heart leaped in fear in her chest.

What happened to me?

Another sharp noise, like a heavy breathing, reached her ears causing them to perk in effort to find the source. She jumped up straight from where she was sitting, realizing for the very first time that she was now standing on something dark and hard which must have been a floor of some sorts. She couldn't see it for the life of her, only darkness.

"Who's there?" She called out, tensing.

A deep growl reached her, making her jump with fright. A flash of light appeared for only a millisecond and then it was gone.

"Please answer! Who is there?" Irene yelled again. Her panic built, making the hair at the back of her neck rise as an uncomfortable feeling settled in the pit of her stomach.

The light she had glimpsed, for only a second before, appeared once more. The growl she had heard sounded louder now, like someone was clearing his throat in a heavy coughing sound. But this time the strange light remained and a tall shadowy form appeared to move with a strange limp towards her. She breathed, somewhat relieved that it hadn't been her imagination. Someone was actually there, and the light she saw in this pitch black room made her exhale much easier now. Feeling herself somehow calmer, she waited for the person approaching her to reach close enough so that she could finally ask what was going on. What had happened to her? Where was she?

The person looked distorted as he moved. Her breath caught in her throat as the form of the approaching man became more clear.

It must've been a man, or maybe it used to be a man.

This was because the form looked like that of a man; however, that is where the resemblance ended. This creature looked horrendous, like someone had burned it out of its skin above a menacing fire, ripping anything human from its previous form. It looked as if the burns had melted its skin away and had glued it upon different parts of its body in horrible wrinkled masses. She trembled at the sight of it and backed away in horror as the creature raised its hand towards her with a moaning sound.

"We are going to have some fun this night." The creature hissed without any sound of reason within it. "We are going to celebrate your arrival, and, oh my, you are a pretty, little thing."

It raised its disfigured hands and tried to reach her frozen face. She was certain her horror showed as she glared at it, feeling her eyes so large they seemed like the would soon come out of their sockets. In panic, Irene squirmed away from the creature's grasp as bony fingers reached out to touch her.

"You will be mine to take and hold and keep this night before the others arrive and spoil you rotten," he said as he moved closer to her. He dragged his feet while making a grimace of a smile. His raw teeth appeared behind burned lips.

He made a move to hug Irene and she quickly backed away in disgust.

"Don't touch me," she yelled, her voice colored in obvious fear as she looked around her for a way of escape.

"Oooooh, but why are you not happy to see me?" The creature drawled out the words as it once again moved closer.

Irene shook her head in dread, her heart pumping strongly in her chest, causing her an unbearable pain.

"Oh my God. Oh my God. Please let this be only a nightmare, please," she screamed, looking around in the pitch darkness that surrounded her. Horror lurked in the depths of her soul.

"A nightmare? What nightmare my pretty? You are here because I called you. You are here because you needed me. You came willingly to me. That is why I found you. Don't you like me?" the creature said, spitting the words to her menacingly as he moved again closer.

"No, no! I don't want to be here! I don't want to be with you. I never asked for this. I don't even know where this is or what I am doing here. I want to go home. I want to go home!" Irene yelled as she squirmed away from the creature's touch, when he reached now for her waist.

"This is your home now. This is where you will stay. Isn't this what you wished for only earlier this night?" The creature eyed her with its strangely unfocused eyeballs nearly hanging out of its sockets and moved again close to her, looking at her expectantly.

"I...I don't know, I... I don't remember doing that." Irene said, in pure horror. *Was it possible I had made this choice?* She looked back at the creature in disgust and her stomach gripped in tight knots.

"Then maybe you should find out because the others will be here soon. They will never let you go back home again." The creature watched her as it smiled in satisfaction.

"I don't understand. I don't know how I got here in the first place. I don't know how to get back," Irene voiced in a crying whisper. Her voice was filled with despair.

"Oh, why would you go now, spoiling my fun?" The creature drawled out as he raised the skin above his eyes where his eyebrows should have been. "You didn't like it back there, remember? You wanted peace and quiet. You were sick back there. There is nothing waiting for you back in that world except pain and sorrow and illness. Isn't that so, Irene?" The creature smiled menacingly now.

Irene contemplated it in shocked silence. *How did it know? Could he read my mind?* She feared him more now and of her dire situation.

"I didn't know any better when I was thinking like that. I didn't mean to come here. I didn't want this!" Irene looked around the vast darkness and felt tears rise upon her eyes.

"Nooooo, nooo, I suppose you didn't." The creature whispered back, as he looked down at her, a glimpse of pity seemed to cross his wide eyes for only a moment before his face changed again into a sickening, deformed smile. "Then all you have to do is take my hand and maybe you will learn to love me and love yourself more for doing that." The creature reached out its bony hand moving his fingers expectantly before her shocked face.

"No, I don't want to touch you." Irene squirmed away again, her dread returning tenfold.

"Oh, but if you do, you might be surprised at what will follow." The creature said smiling again as he moved closer to her with that limping outlandish crawl of his.

More shadows appeared within the light and more growls sounded as Irene looked mortified. The limping shadows moving closer to them now.

The creature looked towards them and turned with a look of impatience in his eyes as he said with urgency in his deep voice, "Quick, woman. Take my hand or you will be forever stuck here."

Irene stared down at his extended, blood stained hand and then looked once more at the shadows coming towards them. She inhaled deeply with rising fear. She closed her eyes as she raised her shaking hand, not wanting to see what she was doing, and then she placed it into the creature's palm.

A soft breeze blew against her face and cold raindrops touched her cold skin while she held the hand of the creature standing next to her. She could hear its breathing and her own, but the other sounds that reached her ears seemed now familiar once again.

"You can open your eyes now, Irene," said a crispy warm voice next to her ear.

~ ~ ~

As she lifted her face, she felt the wind and smelled the rain. She heard a whistling sound from the trees above her as the air traveled through them. Her eyes slowly opened, but she remained silent at the sight she saw. She was standing on her balcony.

The man holding her hand was tall, nearly seven feet high. His hand was warm under hers, and his features where radiant under the light that reached her balcony from the street. His dark blue-black hair shined, his skin glowed smooth and bright, and his beautiful blue eyes were the color of a clear summer sky. His thin lips were softly turned to the corners in a warm smile. His straight nose gave him a tone of grace in contrast with the hard powerful lines around his square jaw. She recognized him immediately, making her heart leap in her chest.

"Paul!" she whispered in astonishment, after seeing her first and only love from twenty-two years ago before losing him in a car accident.

"You did well, Irene. I am very proud of you," he said now looking down at her admiringly.

"What is it that I did?" She inquired in shocked doubt of her very sanity.

"You fought your fears, you faced them, and you chose to rise above them. You left the ugliness of your soul behind, and you once more reached for the light within you to guide you. You did well," he said again, smiling down at her softly.

"I didn't know. I hadn't realized it was you. I couldn't possibly have known," she whispered staring back at him as a bright smile appeared on her thick lips. Love spread within her heart for seeing him again.

"You do have more strength than you believe. You have the light within you. Nobody can take that away from you, except only you can fight yourself on this. You must live, my love. Endure all this life has to give you, and when it is time, I promise I will come for you." He was looking deeply into her eyes, making her feel suddenly very peaceful and warm inside. "Remember this night. You are stronger than what you believe. Everybody is stronger than what they believe," he said in a deep voice as he lightly touched her cheek before fading away.

The cold night breeze blew on her night gown, making her hands and body quiver, but she ignored it now. With raised hands, she looked up in the sky and smiled brightly. She danced with the wind as she called out to the night, "Thank you! I'll remember."

AFTERWORD

By Christine Baely
Author of

Retreating Fog

I wrote Retreating Fog because of a story I heard once about a girl trying to kill herself as she had a fatal illness. It was the mentality that she had at that moment that nothing else mattered for her; neither did she matter to anyone in which this influenced her to make her decision.

In this dream of my heroine, I tried to show the darkness that exists within a person when they decide to leave this world. Nothing else matters to them than except simply finding peace. However, my heroine didn't really have peace in her mind when she chose to do this, and she had to face her fears in the process. The light means hope of the soul, and the mutilated ghost means facing those fears that took her there in the first place. To overcome one's fears means to overcome the fog of the soul, and that is what my heroine does in this story.

Other works that have been published by myself is *The Pradorian Mate*. Two others that are in the process of coming out are *Hidden Leap* and *Soul Light*. I hope you enjoy them all as much as I enjoyed writing them. Thank you.

Shadows
By db Martin

It was warm under there, eyes shut, breathing in his own hot, moist respiration over and over. He clung tightly to the edging of the thick cloth. He shook and his heart beat uncontrollably through every pore of his being. He didn't care though, not in the least, because here, he couldn't see it. No, not here, not beneath the blanket. Here, somehow, he was safe. He knew it didn't make any sense, but it worked. As long as it worked, it would be his sanctuary. It was a nightly ritual: the run. The run from the hallway to the warm bedding, but he knew, he just knew someday he wouldn't make it.

He was christened Joshua David and was born nine pounds and seven ounces, not a small baby by any sense of the word. Once he reached age three, things changed. From that point forward he became a slight sallow child, even bedridden for a while. Now he was continually cursed with insomnia and night terrors to the point that he remained sickly. He was a good child though and never gave his parents a word of trouble except at night. Every night, when nine o'clock came, he was again ordered into the room, and every night, in vain, he fought them on this prospect. He had told them a hundred times why, but they never believed him nor even seemed to care. After a short while, they insisted it was just a childlike ploy to stay up for a little longer, but it wasn't.

Just because you don't believe in something, doesn't mean it's not real. It was there, there in the corner of his room. It was always there. If you walked past it, you may never see it. If you were not listening just right, you may never hear it. It was there just the same. If you looked just right and had your mindset tuned just so, then it all became horribly visible. Once it was visible, it was always there with its constant moans and cries, its strange human-like movements visible one moment then lost within the shadows of the room the next. This faint twilight apparition moved, huddling in the corners of his room, waiting, just waiting.

What was it was waiting for. Why didn't it just do whatever it was going to do and be done with it?

This worry and constant stress of the unknown weighed heavily upon him every night. Joshua would hum, sing loudly, or recite sweet stories to himself, trying anything in insufferable vain attempts to drown out the sounds and formations of mental objects that choked his thoughts.

Joshua lay there, nested in his sanctuary again, listening to the crying, eyes peering just above the hemline of the blanket. He watched the shadow as it writhed and pulled, trying seemingly to work its way tighter into the corner.

"What do you want?" Joshua screamed out, but there was no reply. There was just the consistent crying and sorrowing. He couldn't take it anymore, no, not another night. No more. Joshua tore the covers back and leapt from the bed, now mere feet from this horrific vision.

"What do you want?" he screamed a second time. He took a single step forward, and the shadow twisted and rose, in and out, fading and forming. The moans and cries seemed to grow louder and louder.

"What do you want from me?" Joshua pleaded. "Answer me!" He reached out in an attempt to grab the faded form.

The shadow then rose and fell, pulling itself tighter to the wall, suddenly, within the grey, eyes open wide and staring.

"No!" it screamed, "Go away! You're not real! Go away, ghost. Go away."

"Ghost?" Joshua said, "Ghost?" He looked down at his hands and body, which were almost formless like a shadow in the night, and he screamed!

BEDTIME FOR SAM
By db Martin

"I'm afraid, mommy," Sam said, as his mother entered his bedroom, pulling on her coat. His mom came over, sat down on the edge of his bed, and ran her fingers through his curly hair.

"Sam, you're a big boy now. You're ten years old. I am sorry, but we have to go see Grandma. She's not feeling well. You just got over the chicken pox, so we can't take you with us."

"But I've never stayed all by myself before," Sam said.

"Sure you have, many times."

"Uh-uh, not at night."

"Sam, honey, it's no different. Honest, you will be just fine, and besides, you got Maggie here. Oh, my goodness! Where is Maggie?" She searched around dramatically, in a game they always played at bedtime.

"Where is she always?" Sam replied laughing.

His mom gestured, pointing down – and mouthed "Under the bed?"

Sam laughed shaking his head in agreement.

His mom placed her hand under the bed.

Lick, lick.

"Awe! Maggie, you got me all wet, you silly dog," she said wiping her hand on her pants. Sam just laughed.

"See, you're laughing already," Mom said. "Just remember if you get scared, just hang your hand over the side of the bed, and when Maggie licks you, you will know that everything is ok. Alright?"

"Alright Mommy, I will."

She kissed him on his forehead. "Your Dad and I will be back in about three hours or less, so just stay in bed. If you need us, the phone number is on the wall in the kitchen."

"OK," Sam said with a big yawn. His mom smiled and left the room. Sam sat there in silence listening. In just a few minutes, Sam could hear the car start and the garage door open and then close. He knew he was all alone. He stared at the ceiling for a while, listening to every creak and moan of the house, then he began to get nervous. Sam stuck his hand over the side of the bed.

Lick, Lick.

"Thanks, Maggie," Sam said. "I needed that."

Sam then turned over, pulled the covers up and worked to go to sleep. I can do this, he thought.

Just as he was almost asleep, a noise came from his bathroom. Sam's eyes grew big and he pulled the covers up tighter. He looked over at the bathroom door. It was sitting slightly open, and it seemed just like a black hole carved within his bedroom wall.

"What was that?" he thought as he slowly pulled his arm from in under the covers and let it dangle over the side of the bed.

Lick, Lick.

"Ok," he thought, "Maggie isn't worried, so why should I be?"

"Thanks, Maggie," he said. Then everything was quiet again. Maybe he didn't even hear anything at all.

Maybe he was just falling asleep and thought he heard something. He lay there for a while in the silence and slowly started to drift again. Then "BAM," a noise came again from the bathroom. This time he was sure he had heard it. He stuck his hand again over the side of the bed.

Lick, Lick.

He calmed down after feeling the comforting touch of his dog's tongue on his skin. He could still hear something though. Something seemed to be moving in his bathroom. He slowly pulled the covers down and edged himself over to the side of the bed, never taking his eyes off the black crack in the wall that was the doorway to the bathroom.

Cautiously he lowered himself to the floor. Slowly, step by nervous step, he made his way closer to the doorway. Sam stopped at the door. He could still hear something moving inside the bathroom. He extended his arm and pushed the door open wider. Then he stepped cautiously inside, reaching for the light switch.

CLICK, the light came on.

There lying on the floor in front of him in a puddle of her own blood was Maggie. Her back leg was twitching in a death rattle, kicking the edge of the sink cabinet. He gasped and stepped back. Upon turning, he saw scrawled in blood across the mirror these words:

"Humans like to lick too!"

AFTERWORD

By db Martin
Author of

Shadows
And
Bedtime for Sam

db Martin is an Author, Illustrator and Designer. He lives in Georgia and has been writing for more than thirty years. He has been published in many printed and online magazines.

He has two new books published; "FEEDER - The Blood Chronicles", a Vampire novel and the Amazon Best Selling book "HORRIBLE SANITY" which is a collection of dark poetry.

He has a new book, "MOTHER", which is the second book of The Blood Chronicle series and will be published in late 2016. "TALES OF TERROR", a collection of Horror and his first children's book are slated for 2017.

My New Life
by Andy McKell

It was night. I was asleep. There was no warning.

Something exploded. It was above me or next to me or maybe inside me, I don't know. It was nearby, is all I know - too damn nearby. I jerked up, screaming. Something acid or boiling or toxic sprayed across my face, burning my flesh and melting my eyes. I never knew such pain and I ramped up the screaming enough to rattle the windows, if there was any glass left.

There was a mess of light and fire and thunder all around me. And it was right on top of me. My bed tipped over and I banged my head which stopped my screaming. But I was trapped underneath. That woman started screaming again and that woman was me.

It went on for a long, long time and then it stopped.

But the pain stayed.

It was much later, or not much later - I don't know. I thought I heard movement, but maybe it was my own heart hammering and the blood hissing past my ears. The floorboards shook like a quake hitting. It went on and on and on...

I wet myself. I wanted to scream again but my throat refused to work, I just choked and gagged.

And then it stopped.

Stopped dead.

Silence.

A silence so deep, I thought I was dead. I held my breath in fear till my brain shut down and I slipped out of that hell into a deeper and darker silence that belonged just to me. It wrapped me in its folds and I stayed in that refuge of forgetfulness for I don't know how long.

I woke. I lay cold and wet and shivering in a pool of my own fluids - I could smell it. Someone jabbered insanely. It was me. Then the pain of whatever had slashed my face hit me again and I screamed inside. But the scream was trapped. Inside me. Or I was deaf. Or I was dead.

I didn't scream. Or I did scream and I was deaf. It didn't matter a damn to me which it was. It didn't even matter if I was dead.

Maybe I was dead?

Maybe I'm still dead?

If I'm dead, then being dead hurts and there's never enough to eat and it's always cold - a cold that reaches through to your bones and gnaws on them for hours and locks up your muscles until you can barely shuffle.

We shuffle like geriatrics in loose slippers.

We shuffle like tired, aching souls.

We shuffle like zombies.

~ ~ ~

I'm awake again. I'm lying on the rough ground of a grassy slope. I'm wet with dew. I stink. Everyone stinks. Stale pee and sweat. That iron tang of blood and something else... something sweet and foul. Is my face infected?

I can hear the others coughing as they move about. Something sets the men off. They rage at whatever it was or at each other or at nothing. The women rage at the men.

They are all so angry they just howl and rage, too bone-weary to shape words into insults. Everyone is angry. Everyone is always angry. That'll be the starvation making us irritable. But right now, some of them have enough energy to roar and rage and move about. Perhaps there will be something to eat today, if there's strength enough to forage.

I can smell wood smoke. Will there be cooking or is the forest burning?

"Will there be food today?" It's my voice, but the words are garbled. My jaw doesn't fit my face any more. I'd forgotten. How could I forget?

No-one responds. Maybe no one's close enough to hear me over the raging and howling. Maybe no one cares.

I lift my head to smell and hear better. But there's nothing else, just coughing, snarling and wood smoke. It's so long since I smelled wood smoke.

Maybe I should rip off the cloth clinging to my face, open my eyes, and let the light in?

My fingertips trace the scar lines across my face and pause when they touch fabric. I force myself to imagine clean, hygienic hospital gauze and bandage. But I know it's just a strip ripped from my urine-and-blood-stained bed-sheet. My face must be infected, but I feel no burning. My flesh must be numb from damage or cold or both.

~ ~ ~

There was a raid a few sleeps ago. I think it was dawn; the sound of people waking and moving about and coughing had just started. Without warning, a crowd of screaming somethings charged from up the slope right into us. There was shooting - I didn't know we had guns. I stumbled around and fell and crossed my arms over my ruined face. I rolled away down a slope, clear of the fight. Maybe the attackers thought I was dead. They left me alone, anyway.

I waited until it all went quiet. I heard my folk roar their triumph. It was safe again. And now I could smell food. Meat.

My sense of smell went into overdrive after I went blind. It was my superpower. It was why they kept me. I was useless for anything else.

But why could I smell food? The raiders must have had food. Now it was ours. I stumbled up the slope following the smell of food.

Raw meat again. Do none of these bastards know how to light a fire? We can't live on raw meat forever. Need fruit and stuff. I'd tell them if I could speak properly.

I ate. Raw meat was better than starvation.

After eating, that old longing crept back from where it hid most of the time: a cigarette. Sometimes, I could die for a cigarette. But no one has any. I know they don't; I'd have smelled the smoke.

~ ~ ~

I used to listen for cars, trucks, helicopters… There are none. I'd hear them.

The houses we scavenge are empty. We don't move

at night, so I guess there are no lights. We sometimes cross a hard-packed surface. I stoop and touch it. I'm sure it's tarmac. But there's never a trace of diesel fumes. I'd know; I'd smell it.

No one talks to me. I'm just a nose that picks up the smell of food better than theirs. I smell food, I head for it. They follow me; they open doors; they fight the raiders; they protect me. I'm a nose. I'm a golden nose, I'm a tool. I'm a treasure. I'm a slave.

A slave without chains. A slave without compulsion.

A queen among the dispossessed. A queen among the lost.

No one talks to anyone. Everyone is too tired. There's too much pain, too much hunger, and there's nothing to say. We're heading east; I don't know why. I feel the sun on my face when we head off after waking. No one ever said "Go east" or "It's this way". They were already heading east when they found me. I just followed the sound of their weary shuffling. No one ever said, "Come with us." No one cared if I joined them or not. No one cares about anything except the next meal.

No one has tried to treat me like a woman. I guess I'm no longer desirable, or maybe there's no energy left for sex. I know I don't have enough energy. And I don't miss it. I just want my next meal. My river has dried. I don't know how long we've been walking. It feels like forever. I know I missed a few periods. Starvation and trauma, I guess. It can't be the other. Any fetus would have shrivelled and died. My body can't spare the nourishment for a passenger.

I guess we'll reach the ocean one day or a river or

mountain we can't go around. I don't care. We'll live with it when it happens. Planning needs brainwork. Brainwork needs calories. Lots of calories. Bodies need calories, too. We must keep our bodies going or there'll be no brains anyway. The ocean? I don't care. Maybe I just stopped thinking too hard. Maybe we all just stopped thinking too hard.

I'd wanted a baby someday. I guess that's over. That thought no longer burns in my chest like it used to. I don't think anyone here is ever going to recover enough to give birth or even survive to try. Someone is whimpering. It might be me.

A couple more teeth fell out today. I'm not going to be able to eat meat at all soon.

Now I hear the others shuffling off. I'm aching. Aching inside and out. I struggle to my feet and turn my face to the sounds, to the sun's warmth.

Another day. Another search for food. Another handful of miles closer to the ocean.

I want to die.

But somehow, I don't think I can...

AFTERWORD

By Andy McKell
Author of

My New Life

I wanted to take a fresh look at a rotting subject. How does a zombie feel about its condition? Does it know? Is there truly nothing of them left inside? Anyway, there are so many kinds—fast, slow, alien, brain-dead, quasi-sentient...

Like the government's counter-zombie defense scenarios, my tale does not cover all possible types, so I'll brook no quibbles from anyone who is NOT a zombie. "Queenie" is my zombie. I hope you found her story to be food for thought... brain-food...?

Blog : andymckell.com

The Last Hallowe'en
By Cora Bhatia

The rain pattered against the windowpanes, like the soft pattering of a frightened child padding down the stairs, as she crept into her mother's bed in the dead of night. The wind howled eerily - the night was dark - and bats hung from the dead, withered tree whose long, spindly arms reached out in the night.

Francesca woke up startled, as the windows creaked open - the rain wet her face and bed. She heard tomcats tearing at each other, their screams shattered above the rain, wind, and rattling branches of the multi-hued fall maple trees. The wind tossed the rustling leaves around that made the sound of a snake slithering by.

She stared long at the window and slowly got off her bed. A shadow crossed over the window and then slithered into the darkness of the dead tree. Frightened, she snuggled back into bed under the blanket and pulled it tight over her head.

The rain showed no mercy, now coming in stronger than before, drenching her sweat covered body as the taste of salt and sweat touched her lips.

She thought she tasted blood.

She moved her shivering fingers to her mouth and felt stickiness - she had bitten her tongue and lips in fright.

The nightmare, of the night two days ago, chilled her bones, through the warmth of the blanket and the wetness of the icy rain, which drenched her and the white sheets she slept on.

~ ~ ~

Francesca and her friends had been celebrating Hallowe'en in the forest at an old haunted mansion.

This year, they had decided Hallowe'en would be different - the scariest ever! Her friend, Carmen was born on October 13th and nothing scared her. For her, Hallowe'en, celebrated on October 31st, was the best festival, as if the numbers had reversed themselves to strengthen this fearless nature; she boasted of reinforcing the legend that says if you are born on October 31st you can connect with the dead.

"Let's celebrate Hallowe'en in my ancestors' old haunted mansion," enthused Carmen.

Francesca's friends, Jacob, Phil, Harry, Pamela and Carmen, were all game for the crazy frightful night.

They drove down in Jacob's black Sedan, dressed in their Hallowe'en costumes, faces and bodies painted in vivid colours, some of them in the typical Celtic blue of the woad plant. Carmen and Francesca donned false hair - blood red, mixed with strands of gold. Carmen's reached her knees.

They carried their masks with them and also all the Hallowe'en decorations to make the event real.

The forest was thick and grew thicker as they drove deeper into it. They could barely see the road ahead of them in the car's headlights. Wild animals scurried across their path and they had to keep their eyes focused on the road to avoid hitting them.

Somewhere in the darkness, a wolf howled. The sound sent a shiver down their spines. Out of nowhere, a murder of crows, the harbingers of death, encircled their car. Their raucous screams rent the air, heralding the smell of death and impending disaster.

The massive old mansion, thick with vegetation, and ivy that covered its walls and a large garden, loomed into view. The door screeched open as they turned the key into the lock. The musty putrid smell was overpowering and clogged their nostrils. A layer of dust lay everywhere.

The light of six torches spilled into the room as faces stared at them from the walls filled with photographs. The cold blues eyes of a well-built, bare-chested, Celtic warrior glared at them; his bushy mustache covered most of his face.

A woman smiled back at them. She wore a gold torc around her neck and a long chain that brushed against her well-endowed breasts that almost touched her navel. She was dressed in a colourful tunic. Her cape of thick tweed was pinned with a brooch. She resembled Boudicca, the famous Celtic warrior-queen.

The head of a deer and another of a bear hung on the walls, next to swords and other hunting equipment.

Hurriedly, they switched on the lights. The room lit up with the light of a huge chandelier. They breathed a sigh of relief.

They settled down in the huge living room on massive furniture in rich shades of maroon silk brocade. The dining table, off to one side, stretched from end to end and could accommodate at least a dozen people. Antique lamps and chandeliers were spread all over the room.

"This place belonged to my ancestors, who had royal blood," Carmen stressed.

"That mustached guy must have been a hunter, judging from the animal heads on the wall," responded Francesca, the timid one.

"I wonder if the woman was his wife or mistress," laughed Harry, the cynic.

"I'm sure that man had more than one wife," added Jacob, staring at more photographs of good looking women.

"I don't see any kids' photographs. That's strange," said Pamela who loved kids.

Soon they were into deep conversation as they tried to unveil the mysteries surrounding the old mansion.

Phil and Jacob pulled out the Hallowe'en Jack-o-lanterns and lined the entire veranda with them. They stuck a few in the trees that were in the huge garden at the entrance of the mansion.

The Hallowe'en pumpkins glowered at them in the surrounding darkness. It reminded them of its origin: when Jack first lit a lantern carved out of a turnip to keep away the devil.

Phil had specially created a scary monster scarecrow of corn stalks, dressed in a Hallowe'en costume; he was a mixture of Frankenstein and the Hunchback of Notre Dame. Phil stationed it on the porch of the house. He hoped its presence would scare away any other dark creature from the gloomy forest, amidst which the old mansion was built.

After a quick freshening up, the girls were outside in the chilly dark night.

The boys had already set up the bonfire—that owes its origin to the ancient Celts of AD 60. Celts traditionally used the bonfire as a sacrificial ritual—it meant "bone fire".

The meaning needs no explanation. The ancient druids (priests) were believed to have sacrificed animals and other precious things in this bonfire to satiate the many gods and goddesses they worshiped.

Hallowe'en costumes also originated from the Celts, who disguised themselves in different animal skins and heads to appear as spirits in celebration of Samhain. This was done so that the real spirits would not recognize them as human beings. They would tell scary stories and dance around the bonfire to celebrate Samhain, a Gaelic festival marking the end of the harvest season and the beginning of winter or the 'darker half' of the year.

The Celtic women were as well built as the men and both were warriors and head hunters. They would cut off the heads of their enemies and attach them to the heads of their horses—to be later embalmed in cedar oil and shown off with pride. Stories exist of Celts refusing an equivalent of the weight in gold, as they believed that the head was the soul of the man, the centre of emotions and life itself. They believed it was a symbol of divinity and held powers to the other world.

Jacob, clothed in the traditional Celtic tartan checks, had painted his bare chest and face in blue and purple. Carmen dressed as his Celtic partner and looked like the woman in the photograph that resembled Boudicca, the famous Celtic warrior queen, the chief of the Inceni tribe. The resemblance was spooky! Her thick blood red fake hair almost touched her knees adding authenticity to her look. She even carried an old Celtic sword that she had inherited from her ancestors.

Francesca looked spine-chilling in her black, long cloak of a witch. Her false nails painted a deep shade of blood red. A pointed witch hat, and broom completed her costume. Harry wore animal skins exposing his broad bare chest and a mask of a tiger. Pamela looked hideous in a ghoul costume, while Phil as Frankenstein looked as horrific as his scarecrow.

As they settled around the bonfire sipping their drinks, Carmen asked, "So who is going to scare the shit out of us first?"

Phil accepted the challenge and began his story.

"On a cold winter night, my friends and I entered the cemetery, a little after midnight, on a dare trip to impress Charmaine. She challenged us to place red roses and light candles on her grandmother's grave.

"The silence was dreadful, except for our laughter as we laughed hysterically to ward off the fear gripping our hearts. This was the first time we had entered a cemetery in the dead of night. The eeriness of dead leaves rustling, as we tread silently to the grave of Charmaine's grandmother, sent sweat dripping down our foreheads. We pretended we were not frightened.

"We walked at a quick pace, looking nervously over our shoulders to make sure we were alone. I clung onto the bouquet of red roses, comforted by its sweet moist fragrance against my face. Not a single lamp shed a spark of light. Harry was grateful for the box of candles he carried that we could use to light up the dreary darkness.

"The silence was broken by a harsh voice, 'Whaaat are you boys doing here at night? Are you out of your minds?'

"We saw a bent old man stomping at us and screaming. His left cheek was completely scarred, and he had a limp in his right leg. He looked as if he had not showered in months; his clothes were ragged and filthy.

" 'We...ha...ve...have...come...to...pay our res... pect to... our grandmother,' I managed to stammer out a reply.

" 'At this time of night,' he yelled back, 'go home before it's too late.'

" 'We will lay these flowers, light the candles and go home. We promise,' Harry who was bolder spoke out.

"Still trembling, we lit the candles, placed the bouquet of roses on the grave, and ran out of the cemetery. Our bones were chilled with fright, but the sweat poured down as if it was the peak of summer.

"The next morning, we boasted to Charmaine that we had completed the dare-trip and described our encounter with the old bent caretaker of the cemetery. Her face turned stark white. Her eyes filled with terror as if she had seen a ghost— only it was us who had seen the ghost. We will never forget that look! The caretaker had died ten years ago —found dead one morning, in the cemetery, his face smashed and disfigured.

"Nobody ever found out the cause of his death. People had seen him haunt the cemetery at midnight, warning adventurous youngsters to stay away from the cemetery at night."

Carmen laughed. "What crap! I'm sure you just made up this tale to frighten us. Dare any of you to try out the Bloody Mary legend! I'm sure that's something none of you have ever attempted." Carmen laughed wickedly again.

"No way," protested Francesca. "I've heard that nobody survives the wrath of Bloody Mary. If anyone calls her name three times and lights up candles in a bathroom before a mirror, she comes out of the mirror and lashes out at them, leaving bloody scars. Mary of Tudor was a wicked queen."

"Those are just urban tales told by old maids to frighten kids. I'm sure you guys are grown up enough to at least check this out," objected Carmen.

"I have heard that she spares no one, not even your dear ones. I know of cases, where young kids have lost their lives and been locked in bathrooms that had no locks. They've been found dead. I hear if you say 'Bloody Mary, bloody baby,' she comes out with a bloody child as well," Francesca tried convincing Carmen.

"Okay cowards, I will do this later alone. Now, let's get on with the next tale," Carmen gave up, looking at everyone mockingly.

"Have you heard about the 'Poisoned Hallowe'en Candy' that is supposed to have killed almost a hundred kids knocking on doors uttering 'trick or treat' on Hallowe'en?" asked Harry.

"Yeah, yeah who has not heard of that urban tale of kids being given candy with razor blades, pins, or broken glass also? Tell us something new," Pamela said, laughing at Harry.

"What about the 'Blue Star' tattoo hoax? I believe drug dealers' lace tattoos with LSD that is absorbed into the body just by handling this tattoo. They target school children, making it more tempting by lacing it into popular cartoon figures," Jacob added.

Everyone said they had heard of many of these legends and many more around Hallowe'en, including the Ouija boards, but were not sure if there was any truth in them.

The horror tales continued for some time, each of them trying to outdo the other with their frightening stories.

Finally, they decided to get back into the old mansion and explore it for more thrills.

They put off the bonfire and moved to the porch of the mansion. Nobody noticed the absence of the scarecrow they had stationed there earlier. The other corn stalk decorations of colourful dolls were still in place.

The door screeched open slowly; it seemed heavier than when they first opened it.

"Let's check out the room upstairs. I'm sure it's full of dreary secrets," said Carmen, her hunger for thrills still not satiated.

The stairs creaked and pockets of cold air hit them in their face as the six of them, with torches in hand, climbed the stairs to the bedrooms upstairs. Francesca almost knocked Carmen over in fright, as a big black cat jumped across the long passage, when they were about to unlock one of the bedrooms

Carmen sneered at her, as a wicked smile spread over her face.

She moved ahead and pushed open the door. The stale smell of blood almost choked them. Jacob groped for a light switch, but could not find any.

Suddenly, the lights came on! They saw a headless woman lying on her back, dressed exactly as in the picture of Boudicca, in the living room.

Everyone screamed, except Carmen. The lights went out as quickly as they came on.

Frightened, they backed out of the room, but Carmen focused her torch on the bed—there was no one on the bed.

"Cowards, the bed is empty. Where's the body, see for yourselves," she screamed, half laughing.

Though scared out of their wits, all six torches focussed on the bed. The bed was empty. They laughed at their stupidity.

"Maybe it was just the shadows playing tricks," they thought.

Carmen moved into the bathroom. The others stood at a distance, still not completely convinced. She looked into the mirror, Boudicca's smiling face and gleaming red eyes looked straight at her. She ignored it, thinking it was her own reflection, as she had dressed like the Boudicca look-alike and resembled her so closely.

The group moved from one room to another, as they continued to explore the rest of the mansion. Rats and spiders had invaded most of the rooms. The mustiness, the smells, and the sounds of the innumerable rooms were spooky. But as there were six of them, clinging as close to each other as possible, nothing frightened them as much as the first shock of imagining they had seen the headless body of Boudicca's duplicate.

Exhausted from the night's adventure, they decided

to get some sleep since they planned to move out of the place early next morning.

Pamela tossed around, unable to sleep. She got out of bed and moved into the kitchen to get herself a drink. A shiver ran down her spine as she sensed the presence of someone in the room.

She turned around, terrified, then relaxed and smiled. Carmen stood in the doorway.

Pamela's smile froze on her face forever as Carmen swung her ancestor's sword, slashing off her head. She bent over and picked up Pamela's head. Carmen laughed in victory, like the Celt warrior queen, who had taken over her soul when she smiled at her in the mirror earlier. Her eyes gleamed red. She stuck Pamela's head on a pointed wooden staff.

Pamela's blood spilled all over the kitchen floor—spiders, cockroaches and rats scuttled out of their holes to drink the blood.

The howling of the wolves grew louder. The possessed Carmen walked into the next room, where Jacob, Harry and Phil were asleep—three more heads were added to her collection.

Francesca had locked the door to her bedroom and was fast asleep, since she was under medication. Carmen tried to kick open the door, but it did not budge.

Carmen walked out of the house and moved towards the dead bonfire. She struggled with lighting it.

When the flames suddenly lit, she saw the scarecrow mocking her. The scarecrow had come to life! It bolted at Carmen, picking her up effortlessly as if she was one of the corn stalk Hallowe'en dolls, and threw her into the bonfire, along with the four heads.

Carmen's bones became the final offering to the Celtic gods and goddesses that the spirit of Boudicca's look-alike image had inhabited when she took over the soul and body of Carmen.

Francesca slept through all this terror of the Hallowe'en night.

The morning awakened her to the blood red rays of the sun streaming in through her window and the horrific scene of the blood and bodies of her friends scattered over the haunted mansion.

That was the last Hallowe'en she would ever celebrate. It would always be a day that she would regret all her life! The shadows across her bedroom window and the bats hanging upside-down on dead trees would haunt her every night.

Her blood would curdle every Hallowe'en at the sight of jack-o-lanterns, corn stalks and Hallowe'en bonfires and decorations. Witches, ghouls, and ghosts were now her daily bedfellows, that haunted her dreams and her life.

Afterword

By Cora Bhatia
Author of

The Last Hallowe'en

Hallowe'en to me is an alien festival, as I come from India, where it is celebrated by a handful of people. I have never experienced Hallowe'en, first hand ,and when I was asked to write scary stories of this festival, my first response was, "I am not scared of anything, so how do I write about horror stories?"

This is my first attempt at writing 'Noir Fiction'. I just let my imagination run wild, so I hope I managed to capture the horror that is associated with Hallowe'en and did not overdo it.

I write short stories whenever I need to get away from my main line of work which is editing manuscripts of other writers.

China Doll
By Stephanie Baskerville

"Congratulations, Mr. Sadler. You've purchased a fine cottage there," the realtor shook Johnathan's hand while the ink dried on the papers in front of them.

Johnathan smiled. "Thanks. I think my family's really going to love this place."

"Oh, undoubtedly." The realtor's smile seemed just a trifle forced, but Johnathan remembered the older gentleman's previous comment of feeling unwell and dismissed the oddity from his mind.

On Johnathan's way home, he stopped at the liquor store to pick up a bottle of champagne, then headed to his wife's favourite restaurant to pick up dinner for the family. Since he wanted it to be a surprise, he hadn't told her he was buying the cottage.

"Julie deserves some happiness after losing the twins," he thought, not for the first time. While pregnant, Julie had often talked about how she wanted a cottage on the water for all their children to play and enjoy themselves. When she had miscarried twin boys at twenty-two weeks, it had been devastating for both them and their two daughters. A dark year had followed, but recently, Julie had been hinting that maybe time away from the house would be good for all of them.

That's when Johnathan started looking for a cottage to buy. And then this opportunity practically fell into his lap. Fully furnished, the island cottage was an estate sale with few people interested, despite the amazing location.

Johnathan immediately called the realtor and, within the week, closed the deal. Just in time for the May long weekend.

Driving home, he imagined Julie's face when he told her the good news.

It's been so long since I've seen her smile.

~ ~ ~

"Girls, hold on!" Julie called over the sound of the outboard motor. The boat hit a few larger waves and the girls' shrieks of joy drowned out any other cautionary words. Johnathan and Julie exchanged a look of deep affection.

"I can't wait to see the place," Julie said, clasping her coat a little tighter around her. Despite the sun shining overhead and the late May air, it was chilly out on the water.

"You should be able to see it just as soon as we round this point," Johnathan replied, pointing with his chin ahead of them.

The boat zipped around the point and he smiled as Julie gasped.

"Is that it?" she asked, her eyes alight with surprise and wonder.

"Yep," he nodded, then turned his own gaze for a moment on the cottage.

Cheerfully painted in red, with a black-shingled roof and a large screened-in porch, the two-storey building nestled in among a few trees seemed welcoming and inviting. In front, a painted white dock with blue lounge furniture stood next to a small boathouse that matched the cottage's red and black exterior. White shutters on the windows of both the cottage and boathouse were thrown open wide.

"It's beautiful," Julie said. "Oh, this is just perfect!"

"I'm glad you like it, darling," Johnathan replied.

"I do." She smiled at him. "It's just the place to get our dreams back on the right track."

Johnathan maneuvered towards the dock. The girls, giddy with excitement, helped to secure the bumpers to the side of the boat. Twelve year-old Celeste jumped out the moment the hull lightly kissed the dock with a lead rope that she fed through the galvanized cleat at her father's instruction. Nine year-old Samantha was quick to follow.

As Johnathan shut the boat down, he turned to Julie, taking her in his arms.

"Welcome home," he said, giving her a kiss. From behind them, the girls groaned simultaneously.

"Eew!" Samantha said, eliciting a giggle from Celeste. Johnathan turned around to mock-glare at his girls.

"Hey," he said. They giggled again.

"Mommy and Daddy, sitting in a tree…" Samantha started to sing.

"That's it. Someone's going in the water," Johnathan threatened, alighting from the boat. Shrieking, Samantha ran away from him. With a grin, Johnathan turned and gave Julie his arm.

"Shall we?" he asked.

Exploring the cottage took the remainder of the day. Johnathan was pleased to see the light returning to Julie's eyes and the enthusiasm in her voice as she talked about the upcoming summer vacation.

"I'll get my boating license, so that I can drive the boat when you're in the city working," she said. "And we'll teach the girls how to water ski – oh, I used to love doing that when I was their age."

The girls went nearly wild with excitement when they laid eyes on their rooms. Johnathan had been told that the previous owners had two girls. Sure enough, two of the second-floor bedrooms were kitted out with everything that a young girl, obsessed with princesses, could ever hope for.

"Pretty soon, they'll be begging us to re-decorate their rooms at home," Julie commented to Johnathan, listening to the shrieks of delight from down the hall while inspecting the large master bedroom.

"Whatever makes them happy," Johnathan replied.

"Oh, my dearest… you spoil us," Julie smiled. She wrapped her arms around him and he held her close for a long moment. "I love this place. It's exactly what I imagined when I…"

He looked down at Julie. Tears glistened in her eyes. The stubborn set to her jaw showed him that she was fighting to keep them from falling.

"This place is ours now, Julie," he said softly. "There's still plenty of time left in our lives to try for more children. We don't need to rush anything, but one day, that dream you had will come true."

Julie nodded.

"Dad! Look what I found!" the happy shout from Celeste drew Julie and Johnathan apart. The girl burst into their room, holding a china doll in her hands. She was grinning hugely.

"No fair!" Samantha hollered behind her, obviously upset. "I didn't get a doll."

"Where did you find this, Celeste?" Julie asked.

"She was in my closet," Celeste replied. "I named her."

Julie looked at Johnathan.

"We should probably try to find the previous owners so that we can return this," she said. "It has to have belonged to one of their girls."

"This was an estate sale, Julie. But I can call the agent tomorrow and see if the extended family was ever looking for it," Johnathan replied.

"I want to keep her!" Celeste exclaimed.

"Well, let's see what your father can find out first," Julie said, inspecting the painted blonde hair and blue eyes. "It seems in decent condition. There's a small crack at the back of the head. We'll have to keep our eye on that. Maybe put some glue on it or something to seal it." Julie ran her fingers along the doll's skull. "Doesn't feel sharp, though."

"Can she sleep in my room tonight?" Celeste asked. "Please?"

"I don't see why not," Julie replied. "But you can't sleep with the doll in your bed. China dolls are fragile. They are more used for decoration rather than for playing with. In fact, a doll like this should really be put up on a shelf and left there."

"Mommy, I want a china doll too!" Samantha crossed her arms over her chest and pouted.

"If the family of the owners aren't looking for the

doll, maybe you girls can work something out. It's always nice to share," Johnathan said, giving his older daughter a meaningful glance.

"I'll let you keep her in your room for a couple days of the week, Sam," Celeste said. Samantha's sullen face blossomed into a hopeful smile.

"You mean it, Les?" she asked.

"Sure," Celeste shrugged. "We'll take turns with her."

Much later that night, snuggled together in front of the roaring fire with a glass of wine in hand, Johnathan idly stroked Julie's hair. The girls were both sound asleep, tuckered out from exploring the island.

"I can't believe Samantha wanted to swim today," Julie mused.

"She's half fish, I'm sure of it," he chuckled. They listened to the fire crackle for a few minutes. Then Johnathan heard a thumping noise from upstairs.

Julie chuckled. "Oh, those girls. I wonder which one of them has snuck out of bed."

"I'll go check," he replied. He extricated himself from the sofa's comfortable embrace, put his wine glass down on the coffee table, and made his way upstairs.

Looking in on Samantha first, Johnathan heard nothing but soft snores coming from the bed. There was no way that Samantha had made the noise he'd heard. She was still out like a light. That left Celeste. Johnathan closed Samantha's door and tiptoed down the hall to his other daughter's room. As he cracked open the door, the light from the hallway showed a girl in the bed and the china doll lying on the floor.

Johnathan listened but heard nothing from the bed itself.

"Celeste must have rushed back into bed when she heard me coming up the stairs," he thought, barely able to keep back his laughter. "Now she's holding her breath hoping that I'll think she's asleep and go away."

Johnathan entered Celeste's room and, in the semi-darkness, made his way over to the doll on the floor. He picked it up and, walking over to the bookshelves, returned the doll to the perch Celeste had chosen for it. Then, shaking his head, Johnathan walked back into the hallway, closing Celeste's door behind him.

He was chuckling as he returned to the sofa.

"What's funny?" Julie asked. As he settled himself back in front of the fire, Johnathan told her what he'd found. When he was done, Julie was also laughing.

"That girl. She was probably trying to get the doll so she could sleep with it anyway, even though I told her not to," she said.

"Probably," Johnathan agreed. Content, he went back to running his fingers through Julie's hair.

~ ~ ~

Samantha's terrified screams roused Johnathan and Julie from their slumber.

"Samantha!" Johnathan shouted, bounding from the bed. He grabbed his boxers from the floor and dragged them on, then snatched his robe from the foot of the bed. Julie was scrambling after him, throwing her nightgown and housecoat on with haste.

"Daddy!" Samantha screamed again.

Flinging the door wide, Johnathan saw Samantha in the hallway, staring in horror into Celeste's bedroom.

"What is it?" Johnathan sprinted towards Samantha with Julie hot on his heels. Screeching to a halt, Johnathan's disbelieving eyes took in the sight of his oldest daughter lying upside down, half-out of bed. Her eyes were wide open and a trickle of blood ran up her neck across her face.

"Dear God!" Johnathan shouted. "Julie, get Sam out of here! Go call 9-1-1!"

He raced into the room, nearly tripping over the china doll that was once again on the floor between the door and the bed.

"Stupid thing," he snarled. He snatched up Celeste in his arms. Her body felt much too light, her skin cold, clammy and so pale that it was almost translucent.

"Celeste! Can you hear me?" he exclaimed. "Celeste?"

There was no response from his daughter. Frantic, Johnathan shook her, feeling for a pulse at the same time. Her head lolled limply to one side and his seeking fingers could not find any sign of a steady surge of life within. He shook his head in disbelief. Surely his daughter couldn't be dead. Not knowing what else to do, Johnathan started CPR. Tears flowed down his face. He was sobbing so hard that he often had trouble filling his lungs for the necessary breaths.

It took far too long before the sounds of a helicopter could be heard overhead. Several minutes later, paramedics rushed into the room, carrying their equipment. One took over doing CPR on Celeste while another tried to get Johnathan to his feet to lead him from the room.

"Sir, please come with me. Let us do our job," the paramedic said. Grief-stricken, Johnathan gave in. Julie and Samantha met him just down the hall, both of them crying. As she saw the look on his face, Julie collapsed, sobbing.

"They're working on her now," Johnathan said, his voice hoarse. Both he and Julie knew, though, that Celeste was dead.

~ ~ ~

The paramedics took Celeste's body in the helicopter to the closest hospital for an autopsy. Police officers in speedboats had arrived on the scene shortly after. When they suggested that they would take the family to the hospital rather than having the family drive themselves, Johnathan instantly agreed. He packed Julie and Samantha's things quickly and was ready to leave within the hour. Several forensic investigators were remaining behind.

Samantha insisted on bringing the china doll with her when they left the island. In fact, she'd engaged in such a fit of screaming and carrying on when Julie had forbidden it that Johnathan finally encouraged Julie to give in, thinking that it may at least calm Samantha down and ease some of the grief. Julie reluctantly agreed.

The police were very kind to the family, for which Johnathan was truly grateful. Sure, they'd asked some very pointed questions on the way to the hospital, but Johnathan couldn't fault them for that. He wanted to know just as much as they did what had happened to his daughter.

Mystery upon mystery, however, met them when they reached the hospital. The coroners said that Celeste's body had been completely drained of blood, but yet her body had barely a scratch on her. There were two small pin-pricks about an inch apart on her neck right above her carotid artery, but other than that, nothing else to indicate foul play, nor to explain the massive blood loss. Johnathan allowed their words to penetrate his sub-conscious but barely acknowledged them. He still couldn't believe that Celeste was gone.

Johnathan and his family were given a room at a nearby hotel while the coroners continued their investigation. Figuring that they would never be able to sleep, one doctor provided Johnathan and Julie with mild sedatives. Johnathan refused to take them, dozing fitfully as he listened to Julie's drugged snores from beside him and Samantha's uneasy breathing from the other bed.

Around three AM, Johnathan was awakened from slumber by a thumping sound. He shot up in bed, looking frantically around the room, but in the light coming from the bathroom, could see nothing out of the ordinary. He could hear no sounds from around him.

"Your daughter's just died and you have no idea how it happened. Of course you're going to be jumpy," the logical thought slightly reassured him, and he closed his eyes once again.

But something still plagued him.

"There are no sounds," he kept thinking, over and

over. "There are no sounds."

Gradually, this incessant nagging got the better of him. Rising, Johnathan turned on the light beside the bed. Julie didn't stir beside him, but her back was to him, and with the sedative she'd took, that didn't surprise him.

Johnathan went to the bathroom to splash water on his face. Grabbing one of the cups, he took a long drink of water. Then he returned to bed. His eyes fell on Samantha. Surprised, he noticed her eyes were open and she was staring at him.

"Samantha?" he whispered. "You okay, honey?"

His daughter didn't answer. She didn't even blink. A shiver of foreboding went through his body as he realized that something was wrong.

"Samantha?" he said, louder this time. Still no response. He hurried to her side of the bed, cursing as his foot encountered something on the floor. Looking down for a moment, he saw the china doll lying on its back.

"That damn thing," he thought in the back of his mind, already reaching for his daughter. It was then that he saw the red on her pillow. A thin trickle of blood seeped from two small holes in her neck.

"Samantha!" he shouted, feeling for a pulse. Like Celeste, Samantha's skin was cold and clammy. There was no pulse under his fingers. "Oh God!" he cried. "Julie! Julie, wake up!"

Turning to shake his wife, Johnathan let out a scream of horror. Julie's eyes were also wide open, but unlike his daughters, blood was pouring from her neck. He could see two jagged holes in the carotid artery.

"Oh God!" Johnathan screamed again. He put his hand over the wound on Julie's neck, feeling the life draining from her. "No, Julie, hold on!" he said, reaching for the phone.

Just as he did, something cold and hard grasped his ankle. Shocked, Johnathan looked down. Standing – *standing* – at his feet was the china doll. As it lunged for him, the last thing he noticed was two small fangs, dripping with blood, emerging from its painted red mouth.

AFTERWORD

By Stephanie Baskerville
Author of

China Doll

I must come clean and confess that I can't take full credit for this story. A friend of mine told a version of this story to a group of us at my cottage, sitting around a campfire at 11:00pm one warm July night. I was around twelve years old at the time. I had quite a collection of china dolls and, let me tell you, I sold them all just as soon as I could.

To this day, china dolls still give me the heebie-jeebies.

It was therefore easy for me to decide what I was going to write for this anthology. Something creepy, something that still haunts me to this day – I couldn't resist writing this tale for you! I adapted my friend's version of the story to the one here, so that I could put my own twist on things.

In his version, the china doll is destroyed when the main character smashes it to smithereens, but it comes back to life as he's leaving the island behind forever. It's only at that time that you realize the doll's possessed and it's responsible for the deaths of his wife and daughters. But with this version, I wanted to give you the impression from the very beginning that this doll is somehow sinister. I hope I succeeded.